FLYING WITH ICARUS

Curdella Forbes grew up ~~~~~~~~~~~~~~~~~~~~~
Jamaica, where there was a strong oral storytelling
tradition. She says, "From very early on I had stories
coming out of my ears, long before I was old
enough to discover them in books." Now a teacher
of Literatures in English at the University of the
West Indies, Mona, Jamaica, Curdella lives in Kingston with her niece and an itinerant cat named The
Wild One. She says of *Flying With Icarus*, "It is a book
about how the everyday world is full of marvellous
things, but you have to have special eyes to see them.
Children usually do." Curdella is also the author of
the adult collection of short stories, *Songs of Silence*.

For Mama and Dadda
(Ionie and Sebert), with love

FLYING WITH ICARUS AND OTHER STORIES

Curdella Forbes

WALKER BOOKS
AND SUBSIDIARIES
LONDON • BOSTON • SYDNEY

First published 2003 by Walker Books Ltd
87 Vauxhall Walk, London SE11 5HJ

2 4 6 8 10 9 7 5 3 1

Text © 2003 Curdella Forbes
Illustrations © 2003 Cathie Felstead

The right of Curdella Forbes to be identified as author of this work has been asserted
by her in accordance with the Copyright, Designs and Patents Act 1988

This book has been typeset in Oxalis, Matisse and Artifact One

Printed in Great Britain by Cox & Wyman Ltd, Reading, Berkshire

British Library Cataloguing in Publication Data:
a catalogue record for this book
is available from the British Library

ISBN 0-7445-9067-1

CONTENTS

Slater Minnifie
and the
Beat Boy Machine

The first morning I went back to school after mid-term, there was a new boy sitting in the seat beside mine.

It was Jasper Vernon's seat. Jasper Vernon had fallen off a goods truck and died the term before. Nobody wanted to sit in his seat, so it was really weird to see the new boy sitting there.

He was the fattest boy I had ever seen. He wore round eyeglasses, and he was so fat his face looked like seats. I mean, his cheeks were all raised up and pushed out so they looked like they could sit on. He wore these thick glasses but behind the glasses his eyes squinted, like he couldn't see properly.

I stared. He stared back.

"Hey," I said. "Hey you."

"Hi," he said. He had a small, whispery sort of voice like he was having flu.

"Who're you?" I tried to sound real rough, because Joey Blackett and his gang were sitting in the rows behind me. I couldn't afford to sound too soft, with Joey and them listening.

"Slater Minnifie," the boy said in his whispery having-the-flu voice.

Laughter broke out behind me. "Slater Minnifie? What kind of name is that?" It was Joey, right in the next seat.

Joey's right-hand man Willie Marks started to chant, "Slater grater waiter crater!"

Everton Glass took up the chant from behind him. "Slater hater traitor alligator!"

"Alligator is right!" Joey said. "Hell, man, you ever see anything so fat? Boy, is what swell you? You pregnant?"

The gang hooted with laughter.

"What are you boys up to down there?" Man

Teacher shouted from the top of the room where he was scribbling maths problems on the board and nobody except the girls was paying attention. Joey and his gang shut up quick. They were near getting expelled and couldn't afford to push even Man Teacher too far.

I felt bad. I ducked my head so Man Teacher wouldn't hear me interrupting. "I'm Hylton Blakely," I said. I was vexed because my voice came out whispery, like the new boy's.

The boy sat there, staring straight ahead. For the rest of the class, he didn't speak. When Man Teacher put the new sums on the board the boy wrote for about five minutes in his exercise book. Then he got up and went to Man Teacher's desk.

I thought, Oh boy, this new boy will surely get it now. He won't ever be in any peace from Joey and the gang. For apart from having a weird name and being fat, the new boy was dunce into the bargain. Why else would he get up and take his book to Man Teacher after five minutes? Better he had asked me for help, instead of exposing himself to the whole class.

Man Teacher put on his glasses and looked at the boy's book. Then he took them off and rubbed his eyes. He left a smear of ink all over his face. Man Teacher was the untidiest teacher in the whole school. He always had ink on his fingers like he was working maths problems all the time. Joey said Man Teacher was inky because he never bathed.

Man Teacher looked at the boy's sums after rubbing his eyes, and gaped. Then he put back on his glasses and gaped again. "Good Lord!" he shouted, very loud so everyone knew they were supposed to look up.

Everyone looked up.

"The boy bright. The boy superbright," Man Teacher said. Then he started to shout. "But Jesus God look at this! You send me a genius boy! A boy who solve a whole session of problems in five minutes! Oonu look ya people!" Man Teacher always spoke Creole when he got excited.

And he grabbed his red ink pen and started splashing marks all over the boy's book. Then he held it up for all to see. He had written a great big EXCELLENT! across the page.

Man Teacher was jumping up and down like a Jonkunnu clown and shouting, "Boy with brain! Boy with brain!" The boy stood there blinking up at Man Teacher and looking embarrassed.

Man Teacher was always doing things to make us laugh. He was always shouting "Lawd God, boy with brain!" or "Girl with brain!" when we did something he liked. But this time only some of the class laughed. You could tell people felt funny, because this was something else again. Not even Sarah Miles could do what the new boy did in five minutes. Not even in ten. Not even in fifteen. This boy was from Mars. Joey wouldn't like that at all, at all. I felt nervous for the new boy.

After that, Slater Minnifie got no rest from Joey and the gang, and the rest of the class kept out of his way. Joey's gang was Joey and Willie and Everton and a boy called Deuce Blank because of his two missing front teeth. They became the new boy's sworn enemies. That wasn't no big thing. Joey and them were everybody's sworn enemies.

But the boy was in bigger trouble than everyone else. He was too smart, but not smart enough to pretend to be dumb. Joey and the gang never did any work, and they were really dunce. If you were a boy in the class, you made sure not to do as well as you could or Joey and the gang would take you out.

That meant beating you good and proper in a safe place where the teachers couldn't see, like on the road going home from school. The gang's nickname was The Beat Boy Machine. I always did my best not to get more than 60% on anything. Sixty per cent was all right because it was only average. Joey wouldn't notice you if you got 60%.

Huh! That was what I thought, until I learnt better. Three days before the new boy came, Joey stopped me in the corridor and said, "Hey, Blakely man, I been watching you. Me and the gang. You not a bad guy, you know. We want you in. Think about it."

I was standing with my back to my locker and Joey was standing facing me, crowding me against it. As he spoke, he pulled his ratchet knife from his pocket, very slowly, and flicked it open. Then he smiled, though it was more skinning his teeth than smiling. "Think about it, boyo," he repeated, and moved away down the corridor as the bell rang.

So I was in ba-a-a-d trouble. I had to join or get beat up. I had been beaten by Joey's gang once before, and I didn't want a repeat. I was shaking in my shoes because I didn't want to do the things Joey's gang did to people. Plus, suppose my mother found out? If my mother found me so much as saying hi to anybody like Joey, I was a dead man.

Every day at school Joey was watching me, watching me, to see if I was behaving myself like a boy who was getting ready to join his gang. They had a thing called a test. That meant you had to show you were ready by acting tough. So I had to pretend all the time. I didn't trouble anybody. But I did other things Joey and them did. I shouted in the corridors and laughed loudly in class even when there was no joke.

I got two detentions and my mother was sent for. She was real mad but I couldn't tell her why I was acting weird. I didn't know what to do.

My mother never raised her voice. She just put her voice in a velvet glove and talked soft soft, and you felt like a worm. "Boy," she said. "Boy, let me tell you something. You see how I slaving and killing out myself for you to get an education? If I ever have to come back to this school over your behaviour, dog eat your supper. You understand me?"

"Yes, Mama," I said. I understood Joey, too. That was the trouble.

"I don't know what's wrong with you," she said. "You used to be such a good boy. Now what get into you? You don't reach teenage yet and you already behaving like you stupid. Is what?"

"Nothing, Mama," I said. I couldn't tell her what was really going on because first thing she would go to the principal. The principal would call up Joey and them, and the news would spread. Everybody would know that my mother had to come and fight for me because I couldn't fight for myself.

Those days we all lived in the same community on the wrong side of town. Joey lived two streets down from me. But all I knew about Joey was that he was a boy who was bad from early. And I knew about what happened to his father. Everybody knew about

Joey's father because it was a big excitement in our area.

My mother was one of those parents who never let you on the street late and made you do your homework and mind your own business and keep out of trouble. I saw boys like Joey on the streets. Boys who were men. Badmen. But I only heard about how they lived. Joey and his gang were the first ones I'd met, and I prayed to God I wouldn't meet any more.

Especially as the last two weeks Joey had been getting worse. Was like the devil had got in his insides 'stead of pushing him from the outsides. Twice in two weeks he'd been suspended and was like he didn't care.

In a funny kind of way, the new boy saved me. Joey spent so much time making him miserable, he forgot about me. Every now and then he would still catch me by the lockers and say, "Blakely boy, remember I watching you." And sometimes he'd say, "I expecting you to work on that new boy, you hear?" And he'd skin his teeth and show me the ratchet knife.

The gang wouldn't leave the new boy alone.

"Slater hater traitor alligator!"

"Skinnifie Minnifie! Minnifie Skinnifie! Fatso Watso, wah!"

But the new boy didn't budge. He kept on finishing his work before everybody else and getting everything right, even the really hard subjects like geography and French. He sat at his desk poring over his books, not saying anything to anybody, but sometimes I caught him sneaking looks at me. Whenever our eyes met I looked away quickly.

When the teachers weren't looking, Joey and the gang hit him over the head. The new boy just ducked. He never hit back. Once when he ducked, Joey's hand hit the desk edge instead. "Ow! Ow!" Joey yelled, hopping about on one leg. I bent my head over my book and tried hard not to smile.

"Blackett, what are you up to down there?" Man Teacher shouted, getting up to come and see.

"Nothing, sir," Joey growled. Under his breath he hissed, "Just you wait. I going get you for this. Just you wait till after school."

I don't know if Joey got Minnifie after school

that day as he promised. Minnifie never gave any sign.

The next day, I was struggling over French verbs when I looked up and found him watching me. "Oh, hi, Blakely," he said, stammering a little. "Want some help with that?" He spoke in a half friendly, half ashamed sort of way, like somebody wanting to be friends. Not like showing off at all.

I sat there, not knowing what to say. I thought about how this boy had been at our school for a whole week and hadn't made any friends. Every morning he came in and said "Hi, good morning", I just said "Hi" without looking at him, pretending to be doing work. I always felt Joey behind me, watching.

But today Joey wasn't in school. That was not unusual. Joey was often absent.

The rest of the gang was there, but three desks behind me. They were making paper tails to tie on chairs and attach to the next boy who got up to answer a question. They weren't paying me any mind, for, to tell the truth, they weren't so terrible when Joey was away.

"OK," I said.

Minnifie was really good. He explained the French verbs better than Madame. I took my book up to the table and got all right. I was so glad to talk to him and stop feeling guilty, I forgot I wasn't supposed to get more than 60%.

I said, "Thanks, Minnifie."

He said, "No sweat, Blakely. Any time."

And he went back to his work just as if nothing had happened.

Suddenly I felt all OK, and warm. A weight rolled off my shoulders.

The next day when he came in and said, "Oh hi, Blakely," I smiled and said, "Hey, Minnifie." And we were OK, and he helped me with French again when the gang wasn't looking.

The third day Joey was in school.

All day I felt uneasy. The gang kept huddling together and whispering. I felt something was going to happen.

And I was right. At break time Joey came up to me and said, "So I hear you and Fatty turn big friend, eh? You doing well, man." And he skinned his teeth at Minnifie and me. Then he went away, laughing.

Minnifie looked at me and I looked at him. We didn't say anything. But I was frightened all day. I kept looking at Minnifie but he looked just the way he always did.

That afternoon Man Teacher kept the whole class in late because of misbehaving. By the time we came out, the school grounds were almost quiet. Going through the gate I ran up alongside Minnifie and fell into step beside him. He looked at me in surprise. "Where you going?" he asked.

"I walking with you," I said.

He didn't ask why. He just said, "OK. I take the bus at William Street."

"I know," I said. "I walk home past William Street."

About ten minutes from the school gate we had to pass Mary Brown's corner, which was a lonely part of the road.

Joey and the gang were waiting there for us.

My heart flew into my mouth. I could feel it trying to jump out.

Joey stepped out in the road, blocking us.

"You can't pass," he said, skinning his teeth.

"I passing," I said, frightened and angry all at once. "I passing!" I could hear my voice going up like a girl's. I started to cry with anger and shame.

Joey kicked my shin and I fell to the ground.

I got up on my hands and knees and saw them circling Minnifie. He was just standing there, looking the way he always did. You couldn't tell if he was angry or afraid.

"So what, you not 'fraid, Fat Boy? You not going to run?" Joey sneered.

"No," Minnifie said, whispery like he had the flu. "I not going to run."

"No?" Joey was still circling. "Well, we'll see. We'll just see how long it takes you to waddle out of here. If you can walk by the time I finish with you, Fatso."

Minnifie blinked rapidly behind his glasses. "Beating me up won't solve anything you know, Blackett," he said.

"Solve anything? Who said anything about solving anything? You think everything is math class,

Fatso? You think this is sums we sumsing?"

The gang guffawed.

"No. I meant, beating me up won't bring your father back. Or put the men in jail who killed him."

I can't describe the thing that happened after that. I still not sure what happened. All I remember is that Joey sort of froze, sharp and sudden, like in movies when the camera seems to buck and the picture can't move. His face went all pinched up funny, like somebody held it top and bottom and squeezed it up towards the middle. I didn't know what was happening but I knew something was wrong. I knew Minnifie had said something terrible, beyond redemption, and hell was going to break loose. The gang knew it too, for they just stopped circling and stared at Joey.

Joey opened his mouth and closed it. And opened it again. "What do you know about my father? Who give you authority to talk about my father?" Joey's voice came out at last, all scrunched up and squeaky like mine when I cried "I passing!"

"I not taking authority to talk about your father," Minnifie said. "I just saying I sorry, man. I sorry."

Joey's voice went white. "Sorry? Sorry? Sorry for who?" He was going up into Minnifie's face. I thought he was going to hit him.

Minnifie just stood there looking at Joey, and me and the gang just stood there looking at Joey and Minnifie and waiting for hell to break. There was a funny look on Minnifie's face. He was beginning to look like Joey, all scrunched up like he had toothache.

"I don't say I sorry for you," he said. "I just say I sorry your father dead. That's all."

Joey hit him then. He hit him in his belly and it sounded like somebody slapping a wet cloth on stone. Minnifie bent over, holding his stomach, and sat down on the ground. He looked up at Joey, still not saying anything, and Joey began to cry.

I was really frightened. It happened so suddenly, it felt unreal. Joey's face just twisted up worse than ever and a horrid sound like whooping cough came out of him, and he held his stomach and began to cry.

"Hey, Joey," Deuce Blank said. His top lip lifted like a squirrel so you could see his no teeth. I'd never seen Deuce looking frightened before.

Joey turned on him like a madman. He cursed a bad word and then he was shouting at us to get out of there and we were so stunned, we just went. Some others from the class had stopped to watch but to tell you the truth I was so dazed to see Joey crying, I don't know if they went too or if they stayed to watch the rest of what happened or to laugh. I really don't know.

I waited for Slater at the bus stop but he didn't come. I went back up to Mary Brown's corner, shivering all the way, but nobody was there so I went home. I was scared all night, I couldn't sleep.

Next day Joey was absent again. But there was big excitement and it was all over the class that Minnifie made Joey cry. I asked Minnifie what happened after we ran, but he wouldn't tell me. All he said was, "Blackett's going to be all right, you know."

"How you know that? You is Jesus? You is St Paul?"

"Yes, well."

"What you mean, yes well?"

"I mean, he didn't mean to do all those things, you know? He just wanted to do something for his father. I think he just wanted to do something for his father."

I was sure Minnifie was mad.

"Did he beat you up?" I asked.

"No," he said.

"You beat him up?" I knew the question was ridiculous, but I asked it anyhow.

"Blakely, man," Minnifie said. "You know I can't fight."

"How'd you know about his father?"

"Everybody knows about his father."

"Yeah, if you live in the area."

"I live on Bond Street."

I stared. He didn't seem like anybody from our part of the world. He behaved like somebody from Mars. I just stood there thinking how we all lived in the same place and we didn't know each other.

In a sort of way, it was my mother who made me understand about Joey's father. That weekend she was reading the death notices in the *Star*, the way she always did. She liked to read them to see if there was anybody she knew.

Suddenly she said, "Oh. It's the anniversary of that man they kill. See they have memoriam in the paper for him."

"Which man?" I asked.

"That man where they never found the killer. You know. The one with the boy that turn bad." She read out loud. "'In loving memory of Arthur Blackett, departed today 24/4/01, one sad year. In tragic circumstances. We know not Lord what thou dost do but all is well that's done by thee.'"

I grabbed the paper from her and looked. It was a big notice in the middle of the page.

There was also a big photo of Joey's father. He looked just like Joey, only older, and he had a beard.

Right below that was another notice, much smaller. "In memory of Daniel Minnifie. Departed 6/4/01. Rest in peace. Sadly missed by loving wife Jada, daughter Isabel, son Slater."

I stared at the page for ages, thinking about Joey and Minnifie and death and dying, and

Minnifie and how he seemed to understand things like a man who was old. Things about acting mean from hurting because your father died, and paying people back for your hurt even though it wasn't their fault. I thought about how Minnifie didn't hurt anyone for his father dying, yet still he understood about Joey. And I thought about how we all lived in the same place and didn't know each other and I didn't even know Minnifie had a father and that he died. I sat there for a long time thinking about these things and then my mother said get up it's time for bed, and I got up and went to bed.

Seashells

I was going down Breadnut Hill on my way to Saturday market when I heard a big commotion and saw a crowd of people round a big hospital-looking van parked at the roundabout. Somebody flashed past me yelling, "Whoi, whoi, people, run come here! See they putting Lena inna 'sylum van! They putting Lena inna 'sylum van!"

It was my best friend Clancy's mother's sister. Two twos, before I could draw breath, Clancy herself brushed past me like lightning. "Come on, Annette!"

After her, a whole crowd of people started

coming out of their yards, running towards the van. I ran after everybody else just in time to see two policemen hoist Lena into the van and slam the door shut.

Lena's face looked out at us through the window. It looked the way it always did, like a clown's mask, all white with powder, and three red slashes on her mouth and cheeks. But this time she looked angry. It was the first I saw Lena look anything but serene. She looked like a ruffled whitefaced hen. Even though I was puzzled and scared, it made me want to laugh.

"What they taking Lena away for?" I asked Mr Glenn, who was standing next to me. "What she do?"

Mr Glenn didn't answer. People were surrounding the van and shouting and refusing to move. The policemen waved batons but still the crowd didn't move, and more people were coming.

"What you taking her away for, Officer? What she do?"

"So, you recruiting madpeople now for the police force?"

"But Lena don't trouble nobody! Look how much years now she peaceful. How long she mad on the street and peaceful."

But the policemen shoved some people aside and got in the van and drove off.

Miss Prescott's son Peril, whom everybody called City Puss, shouted, "But this is thiefery, you know! Thiefing the woman from off the street like that."

Some people laughed, because everybody knew City Puss was the biggest thief in town. That's why they called him City Puss, because he stole worse than a cat, but in big style. City Puss stole fit for a city, not a small market town.

A policeman stuck his head through the window and shouted back, "So she belong to somebody? You want me to pay you money for her?"

Lena was sitting in the window looking at us with that comical, annoyed look on her face. When the van got to the corner she waved, slow and regal, like an African queen. It was like she thought she was in a movie and somebody should take her picture.

People started quarrelling and saying how the police was so rude, somebody should put a stop to them, and how they can come in the town and move out a madwoman without saying anything to anybody? There were some people who didn't belong to the town but had just come in to do their business. They said the same.

But the van was gone, so there was nothing anybody could do. Mr Glenn, who lived on the avenue by the police station, said he would go down there and investigate, but he couldn't do it now because he was fixing shoes in his shop. Everybody was busy because it was market morning, so people just grumbled a bit more and said, "Awright Mr Glenn, you check it out and mek we know," and went back to their business.

Nobody believed Lena was in any real danger. They were just mad at the police for bad manners and not satisfying their curiosity. Lena had been our madwoman for ages and ages. Everybody knew her, including the police. We knew it was nothing serious and they would bring her back.

I hurried up quick quick to buy the things Aunt

Vera sent me to buy because I didn't want her getting mad for I was staying too long.

But the police didn't bring Lena back. In the evening we heard on the news they were rounding up streetpeople and taking them to safe places where they could be looked after. Apart from Lena, they had rounded up lots of people in the parish and taken them in.

People in Lucea town were hopping mad.

Aunt Vera never paid Lena any mind, but now she said, "Streetpeople, which streetpeople? You see Lena is any streetpeople? Look how long Lena live among us mad as shad and we taking care of her and she not troubling anybody nor causing no nuisance to government! Streetpeople what? Streetpeople where?"

Clancy and I didn't know what to think. Lena was like fixture in Lucea town and we couldn't imagine passing the leaking hydrant on our way to school or going by the beach and not seeing Lena. What the people said was true. Lena was mad longer than for ever, but it was a nice mad.

She was tall and stately with fair skin and lots and lots of hair which she coiled in a bun and pushed under a neat jippy-jappa hat with silk ribbons. She was always dressed neat and squeaky clean in long straw-coloured skirts and matching blouses. She had all these rows of pale-coloured beads around her neck. She pasted white powder on her face so thick it looked like somebody had their face in a cast. On top of the powder on her cheeks and lips she plastered red red rouge and lipstick like blood.

Lena never troubled anybody. She just used to come out every morning with her straw basket on her arm, full of bathing things, and stop at the leaking fire hydrant in front of the post office and wash herself and put on her makeup again. That took her from dawn to about nine o'clock.

If you passed by her she said, "You bathe since morning?"

If you were stupid enough to answer, "Yes, Lena," and stand, she would say, "Is true? Mek me see in your nosehole," and she would grab your face and peep down into your nose.

You had to say, "Yes, Lena," and run.

The hydrant wasn't the only place Lena washed herself. She liked to have another set of wash at midday, but by then the sun was real hot, so she went down to the sea. During school holidays Clancy and me saw her by the beach a whole lot, because we were always going there to look for shells and coloured rocks and kick our feet in the breakers and sometimes, when no adults were looking, swim out to the buoys.

Lena was almost always there. She used to stand at the edge and throw seawater on her face, dry off, then make up again. Then she would walk out into the water and come back up the beach gathering shells, like us. She had this habit of putting the shells to her ears and then putting them in front of her eyes and shaking them and hissing her teeth, then flinging them away. It was like she was listening for something in the shells that she never heard.

If she saw us gathering shells, she hissed her teeth and said, "Lef the shell alone. Idiot. You bathe since morning?" And Clancy and me'd laugh and I'd run. Boldface Clancy didn't run, she just cocked her bottom at an angle and went sideways like a crab so if Lena tried to grab at her nose she could run. Lena noticed Clancy was set to run so she never troubled her. But one time Clancy with her boldface pushed up her hand and poked Lena's face to see if it would come off, and Lena lifted her basket and swatted Clancy one swat on her hand with it.

"Rude," Lena muttered, sounding like Aunt Vera scolding. Clancy yowled and sucked her bruised knuckles. She never touched Lena again, but still she didn't run. Mostly Lena just ignored us, gathering shells and walking in the sea. When she'd satisfied herself, she'd climb up the beach back into town. By sunset she was back at the hydrant, washing her plaster-cast face again.

People in restaurants gave her food. Aunt Vera said nobody ran her out of the restaurants because Lena knew how to be a lady. She carried herself like a queen. She liked to clean the restaurant people's bathrooms in return for her food. The bathrooms didn't need any cleaning because the people had workers to clean them. But Lena cleaned them anyway.

One time Clancy and me went in the Kentucky Fried Chicken bathroom and Lena came in.

"You flush the toilet?" she said in her gruff voice that didn't fit her whitey-whitey appearance.

"Yes, Lena," Clancy said, though we hadn't used the toilet at all. We went in to try out Clancy's new lipstick that she bought and hid because we were too young. Clancy just wanted to see what Lena would do.

"Let me see," Lena said, and opened the toilet door. I got scared. The bathroom was a confined space. Suppose she decided to hold us down and look in our noses? Lena was tall and big and I was little and skinny and Clancy wasn't so big either. I turned tail and ran. Clancy ran after, but she was mad.

"You wouldn't even wait to see what she go do!" she accused me angrily. "I wanted to see if she would wash her face in the toilet water. People say she wash her face anywhere she see water."

"Yuck!" I said, disgusted more with Clancy than Lena. But I wondered how come the skin on Lena's face never peeled off with so much washing. Maybe it did. Maybe that's why she put the powder cast on.

The day after they took Lena away hell broke loose in Lucea town and Mandeville. Mandeville people came out on the streets demonstrating because a whole tonload of streetpeople suddenly appeared on their clean clean streets where was no streetpeople before. Nobody could tell where they came from. Lucea people started to demonstrate because Lena's people came out in the town cussing and swearing to prosecute whoever took Lena, and they had better bring her back. So the townpeople went and joined them.

That was when Clancy and me knew that Lena had people. We always used to wonder where she came from. We figured she must live with somebody to have such nice clothes and look so neat, even though she washed at the fire hydrant. It turned out her people lived in Granville and every morning Lena got money to take the bus so she could do her daily work washing herself at the fire hydrant.

"I guess it keep her occupied," Clancy said facetiously. "People say having no work can drive you mad. They don't want her to get mad."

"You idiot. Lena mad already."

"Not really. She just quiet."

"So because she's quiet, she can't be mad?"

"Huhn-huhn. But not Lena. You ever see mad person so neat?"

"Maybe she a neatness freak. Maybe that her kind of madness."

"Or maybe she tired how the town damn dirty. After how many years she can't get nobody to follow her example. She will be glad she reach at clean cool Mandeville."

"Mandeville can't suit Lena. It don't have neither sea nor river."

"It have fire hydrant though. What the hell Lena doing with sea and river?"

I hissed my teeth because I could see Clancy just wanted an opportunity to swear "damn" and "hell", and now she got it. I ran off and left her and went to join the demonstration.

The demonstration was sweet because people

dressed up and painted their faces like Jonkunnu and played loud music and waved funny placards. One lady had a placard that said, GIVE WE BACK WE MADPEOPLE. EVERYTHING YOU ALL SEE POOR PEOPLE HAVE, YOU WANT IT. I got to dance to all the nice musics Aunt Vera would corn me if she caught me listening to. It was like Christmas.

But the demonstration spread and got nasty. This is how it went.

Some people from the Citizens for Justice and the Society for the Prevention of Cruelty to Streetpeople came, and TV with big cameras. At first it was funny. The TV people asked a fat lady why she was demonstrating. The fat lady laughed and said, "I don't really know, you know, sar. I passing and see the excitement so I join it too." She skinned her gold tooth wide wide for the camera. Later she must was happy because it came on TV.

The TV people asked the Citizens for Justice and they said a lot of things I didn't understand about injustice to streetpeople and streetpeople rights and how the streetpeople would suffer from being displaced. Clancy pushed herself up in front when they were taking the Citizens for Justice lady's picture. She wanted to come on TV too. The police came and threw teargas and Clancy got some in her mouth and was sick for days. She didn't come on the TV.

In the end the government got in trouble because the TV people found out the police took out all those streetpeople to clean up Lucea town and took them to mess up cool clean Mandeville. They didn't take them to any safe place at all at all. The government had to promise to investigate. The police got in their vans and went and got back most of the streetpeople and put them on the street again.

But they didn't bring back Lena. Lena couldn't be found.

Clancy said, "Let's go and ask the Citizens for Justice and the Prevention of Cruelty people to help find Lena."

"Who, me? No way, José."

I wasn't going anywhere with madhead Clancy. No way was I going to these people to show off so I could be told I was just a child and to leave bigpeople business alone. I was always having to rescue Clancy from all sorts of ambitious schemes. I never knew a girl so, always trying to act like she was big.

Furthermore, the Prevention and Citizens people were busy. After most of the streetpeople came back, a big advertisement from them appeared in the newspaper saying JUSTICE HAS BEEN SERVED. WE STAND FOR THE PEOPLE. The Citizens and Preventioners had a big rally commemorating the anniversary of the streetpeople's return. They put on a big streetplay showing how it had all happened, how the streetpeople were taken away and how they were fought for and returned. The head lady was a very good actress and it was really great fun to watch. I couldn't believe how they made the baglady and drughead costumes so realistic.

Then one day, long long after all the excitement died down, I was sitting by the sea and Lena came.

I was sitting there feeling sad because I had to go away to boarding school, and Clancy was staying.

I was there wondering what I was going to do without my best friend.

"You bathe since morning?" a familiar voice said behind me.

I turned around faster than light.

She looked different. Her clothes were tattered like she hadn't changed them for a long time. You could see they had been washed over and over but they weren't very clean. She didn't have her jippy-jappa any more and her hair needed combing. It looked like she had tried, but hadn't done a good job of it. She also didn't have her straw basket with the cleaning things in. She had a conch shell. It was white with blue streaks like veins. I wondered where she got it from. There were no conch shells on this beach, so she must have got it from wherever she was coming from.

"Lena!" I cried, so relieved I forgot she was mad. "Lena, where you come from? Where you was?"

Lena stood over me looking down. "Face want wash," she said disapprovingly.

It was true. I had been crying and then I wiped my hand in the sand and wiped it in my face. I could feel the sand grains like rough, sticky tears.

I laughed. "Is eyewater, Lena," I said. "It fossilize on m' face."

Something seemed to connect because she jumped like somebody had come to arrest her again. "Eyewater? Eyewater? What you have eyewater for? Anybody trouble you?"

I didn't know Lena had so many words in her head. Suddenly it didn't feel stupid to be talking to this madwoman. "I going to boarding school and I go miss my friend," I told her, like I was talking to somebody real. "But where you come from, Lena? Where you was all this time?"

She was looking at me like she was hearing something else. "Who trouble you? Somebody trouble you? Here, tek this." She pushed out her arm in a sudden way, all jerky, and gave me the shell. I was so surprised I took it before I realized.

Lena gazed at me earnestly. "Listen up," she said. "Hold it up and listen up. World in there."

I put the shell to my ear and listened. I heard a sound like the sea was inside and it was so soft and whispery and wonderful and sad, I wanted to laugh and cry and fall asleep and run all at the same time. Lena watched me anxiously for a while. I closed my eyes to hear the shell better, but I could still feel her watching me.

Finally she squatted down beside me. "World in there. Lena listen, Lena listen. Lena listen and follow the sound come back home."

"You mean when you were there in Mandeville, where it don't have no sea, is the shell show you how to find back here 'cause it tell you to walk by the sea?"

Lena looked at me blankly as if I was mad. Then it looked like she lost focus, for she just got up and walked out into the water far away from me. I sat there watching her and listening sometimes to the waves in the sea and sometimes to the sea in the shell.

After a long time she came back up to the beach and she had a lot of little shells in her hand. I held out her big conch shell and said politely, "Thank you, Lena, that was very nice."

"Keep it. You don't want it?" Lena looked disgusted. Then she said, "Lena reach home now.

Keep it. Idiot." Then she hissed her teeth and went up the beach into the town, leaving me holding the shell.

When I left I took Lena's shell with me. Nights when I felt really homesick I sat up in bed in the dorm and put it to my ear and listened to Lena's world of the sea. It made me feel better.

Nobody ever found out how Lena got home from Mandeville. But when I told Aunt Vera about the shell, she agreed with me that maybe Lena found or stole the shell somewhere and it somehow reminded her of where she came from, so she just walked along the coast roads until she got to where she recognized.

We will never know. But the journey and the shell seemed to change Lena in some way. I guess the way going to boarding school changed me. Aunt Vera said it was all part of growing up. I guess we both were growing up, Lena and me.

Clancy wrote and said Lena was OK again. Her people in Granville took her back in and she had new clean clothes and a new basket and fresh rouge and lipstick. Redder than ever, Clancy said. But she didn't wash by the fire hydrant any more. Now she washed only in the sea. Clancy said any time of day you went down by the beach you could see Lena, either washing herself or walking along the shoreline combing the beach for shells. It was like she felt she had lost the sea that time they took her to Mandeville, and she didn't want to risk losing it any more. Maybe she thought if she stayed by it all the time, she could keep it from going away, Clancy said.

I just hoped she found a shell with worlds inside, like the one she gave me. Because at boarding school whenever I was lonely, Lena's shell made me feel like I was safe and coming home.

THE MAN WHO LOVED FLOWERS

"**D**on't go up at Cappi John house," my mother said, warning. "If I catch you setting foot on even the grass there, corn I corning you."

"Corn I corning you" meant she would lash us good and proper.

My father, who usually left such things to my mother, said, "Hear what your mother say, boy?"

"Yes, Dadda," I said meekly, wondering when I could go to look what was the excitement at Cappi John's place.

Cappi John was an old man who walked on his

ankles. Something twisted him at birth so his feet turned in, like kissing peas. Isaac and me used to shoot birds by his house, every summer when school was out.

Even when yucky school was in, we went by Cappi John. Cappi John made toto cakes and sold them in a big ground-basket. He carried it on his head, singing, "Toto, toto! Sweet toto cake!"

But then he died. He was old. Though when you saw him he didn't look any age.

We missed him very much. Isaac cried with rage and wouldn't eat for days.

Cappi John was just different. He treated us like we were grown and gave us advice about life and women and how to catch fish without a fishing line.

He never told on us. Even the time we tore the plank out the side of his house. We went inside through the hole left by the missing plank and borrowed Cappi John's knife to peel breadfruit for our secret cookout. My mother locked up her knives because she said we would hurt ourselves one fine fine day.

We put the knife back and we thought the plank wouldn't show where we had moved it, because it was falling down anyway. But Cappi John saw. We forgot he had eagle eyes because in his young days he was a tailor, like my Uncle Hannan. That day he was in a bad mood so he started quarrelling about his houseside. He went down the hill shouting as he went, "But you see idle boy bruk into me house, oh? Eh, eh-eh, eh? Bruk out the plank and bruk into me house!" Cappi John got so excited he forgot my mother was hearing him. "You see the persecution? You see the wickedness? Bruk into me house and thief out me plank!" Cappi John was getting so excited, he got confused. He thought it was the plank we took, not the knife.

I wanted to correct him, but I kept quiet because my mother was standing listening. Her eyes started to cross and her eyebrows started to gather like well-tight crochet. She held down her head looking at me and Isaac like she wasn't looking. I knew if we tried to run we would get it, because my mom was putting two and two together and making four. Even though Cappi John wasn't calling any names.

We realized how upset he was because usually he would just call us and say, "Boy, is you tear off me plank? Pay two grand, pay two grand." Of course he knew we didn't have any money to pay him, but that was just his way of telling us we should set things right. So we'd apologize and help him fix it back, and that would be the end of that. Our mother would never know. Even now when he was mad he was careful not to call names.

But my mother suspected us if a neighbour coughed and said maybe they got pneumonia from somebody. We couldn't blame her. We had a knack for trouble, all the grownups said. Mostly it was because of Isaac. Isaac was daring. Doing things with him, I felt great and famous.

By the time Cappi John finished shouting, my mother was coming at us. "Don't run, boy. If you run, I corn you worse!" We ran, of course. But in the night when we crept in through the window thinking she was asleep, she wasn't. She got up and corned us worse, tons of lashings for Cappi John's plank.

We didn't hold it against Cappi John. The next

evening when we went by him he said, "Sorry, sorry, gentlemens." Cappi John was always polite. He said he learnt it in the army when he was in the war. My mother said it was a lie because no war would hire Cappi John with his twisted feet. We believed Cappi.

"Sorry, but I was real cut up 'bout that plank, I forget myself. Never mean to betray you to your mother."

"'At's all right, Cappi," Isaac said generously, speaking for us both. "No hard feelings. A man got a right to vex sometimes."

"Yes, a man got a right to vex sometimes," Cappi said. "A man really mustn't provoke a man too far, eh? Specially when a man poor and can't buy board to fix up his falling down house, eh-eh?"

"Yes, Cappi John."

"So man and man all right then, awright sirs? No hard feelings from me to you or you to me, eh-eh?"

"No, Cappi John. Cool, Cappi."

And on that we shook hands.

That was the kind of man Cappi was. He was our hero.

After Cappi died, his little house was locked up for a long time. Grass grew all over the yard until the house looked drowned. People let goats in and they messed in the grass, so it looked full of black gravel. But still the grass grew and more of the planking fell down. We felt real sad.

My mother couldn't manage us that summer. My father didn't care. So my mother sent us to town to stay with Aunt Beatrice and Uncle Sammin. They got tired of us and sent us back early. And when we got back, there was our mother saying, "Don't go up to Cappi John's house or I corn you."

And my father agreeing. Wonder of wonders. Something had to be in this. We were going to see.

As soon as my mother's back was turned Isaac looked at me and I looked at Isaac and Isaac said, "C'mon, let's go." We held hands and ran all the way to the hilltop.

We nearly dropped down. Isaac's mouth opened and shut like a half live fish. I fell on my knees in the high grass, panting. I had to draw breath after our fast run up the hill and now this.

"Jesus God," Isaac said, reverent like the wickedest sinner.

"Jesus God," I echoed, waiting for Isaac to say the rest.

"Somebody take over Cappi John house." Isaac was whispering, like he wanted to cry.

"And fix it up," I said, whispering too because I didn't want Isaac to cry. I didn't know if he was mad that somebody took over the house, or glad because it looked so smashing. Smashing and happy like it would never ever fall down and die.

The grass was cut and flowers and new trees were everywhere. All kinds of flowers. Red and yellow and orange and purple bougainvillaea. Red and pink and white hibiscus. June roses and some white stuff like stars whose name I didn't know. Cactus and yellow coolie lace and stinking toe so bright it hurt your eyes. Little baby roses like silver and blood. Kinds of trees I never saw in my life before, but one was a rubber tree like in Aunt Beatrice's houseproud yard in town. It looked like an enchanted garden.

Somebody had painted the house pale yellow

with green trimmings and it ought to have looked silly but it didn't. It looked nice. The sides had been repaired, new planks and everything.

"I going into this, boy," Isaac said. "I going to find out who have this. Come on, Ishmael."

Only Isaac called me Ishmael. Everybody else called me Ishi. They said my mother took a joke too far, calling me Ishmael and my brother Isaac, like there was a curse on me. Like Ishmael in the Bible, who had to run away because his brother Isaac was born. But I didn't mind. I liked my twin brother being the only one calling me my right name.

We shouted but nobody answered. We tried the door but it was locked. It had a real lock instead of the wooden latch Cappi used to have on it. We were trying to pick the lock when somebody shouted, "What you all doing? Come out of that place right away."

It was Uncle Tir, coming from his banana field. Uncle Tir was really Mr Terence McDonall. He wasn't anybody's uncle, but everybody called him Uncle Tir. We moved away from the door quick quick, hoping he hadn't seen us trying to pick the lock.

It looked like he hadn't.

"Come away from there, come away from there." Uncle Tir was looking stern. "Not a good place for you to be in, boy. Go home. Go on home to your parents now now, and don't come back here."

I was ready to scuttle but Isaac wasn't letting go. "So why, Uncle Tir? What wrong with the place? Who live there now? Everybody telling us to stay 'way from there."

Uncle Tir spat on the ground. "Whoever live in there not good for you to know, boy, go on home."

Isaac started to protest but Uncle Tir got vexed, so we left.

We couldn't understand it. How could somebody be bad who made all the gardens we knew look like chicken runs?

We went down to Newton Johnson's house and collared him. Newt was in his yard pitching marbles with his little brother Cuthbert and his sister Geraldine with the teeth like Zero in the Beetle Bailey comics.

"Who live up at Cappi John house?" Isaac said.

He put his big toe in front of Newt's marble so he couldn't pitch and had to answer.

"Man, how I must know, man? You think I is Miss Nellie?"

Miss Nellie was the district's cable and wireless. If she knew anything about you, you had to cry "Mouth, have mercy!" Miss Nellie talked everything.

"Is a man from outer space," Cuthbert said, shooting out his mouth and sucking his finger.

"What you mean outer space? You a idiot, boy?"

"Don't call my brother no idiot," Zero-face Geraldine cried, ready as usual to fight.

Isaac ignored her. Cuttie went on sucking his finger and feeling his navel under his shirt. He had this slow, thinking look on his face, so we knew more was coming. We waited.

At last Cuttie took his suckfinger out his mouth with a loud *pop!* and said, "Me muther say he is a black art man. Say you mustn't go over there, he wi' cut out your liver."

I stared. "How you mean black art man? What

black art man doing in Baltree? Where he come from come here?"

Cuttie spit in the yard like big man. Geraldine thumped him. "Don't spit in the yard. You don't hear Mammy say don't spit in the yard?"

Cuttie kicked out at her and she skipped backwards. "Heh, I go tell Mammy you kick me! I go tell Mammy you kick me."

Cuttie ignored her. "They say he work for D Lawrence," he said, not answering Isaac's question.

"D Lawrence?" Isaac looked scornful. D Lawrence was the world's biggest international obeah man. He lived in America and he could turn your mouth behind you or make you walk on graves at night. Isaac didn't believe a word of it. Isaac didn't believe about Santa Claus either.

Seeing he wasn't going to get to play any marbles for now, Newt spoke. "Nobody don't really know where the man come from, yah," he said. "He just come here one night out of the blue and take up residence in Cappi John ole house and start fixing it up. He don't look like anybody from round here. He drive one fancy Mercedes car and every day since the last two weeks he start driving out early morning and coming in late o'clock night."

"What man in Mercedes doing in Cappi John ole house?" Isaac demanded. Our district was poor, Cappi John's house was a two-room board house, one of the poorest. People with Mercedes lived in Cherry Gardens in town, not in a two-room in Baltree.

"How I must know?" Newt said, vexed. "You see me reading crystal ball?"

"Mammy and Pappy say we not to talk to him becausen he entice children with sweetie," Gerald-ine said behind me. Looked like she didn't like to be left out of man-talk.

"Who he entice?" My brother, strict as any judge, wanted the full and only truth.

"Nobody," Newt say. "At least, not as far as I know. When he just come, he use to stand at the fence and call out good morning to all who passing, and asking the children what they name and giving them sweetie, though he quarrel when they thief he pretty flowers. But my mother say something funny, because town man don't usually so polite. Look like he study country people ways and know we like good morning and good evening, so he just doing it to fool people. But he overdo it, man."

"When they ask him where he come from he say 'up the line'," Geraldine say. She spat like she was mocking. "Anywhere from Mocho Pen to Timbuctoo. So we know he is a funny man. Something not right. What he have to hide?"

That was what we were going to find out. The next few days we scouted out the ground by Cappi John's place. We took care to hide in the bushes so no adults could see us. No other children came. Everybody walked wide of the house when they passed.

We took care not to say anything, so our mother couldn't see we were interested. It didn't work – she just got suspicious.

"You boys hanging out by Cappi John place?"

"No, Mama."

"Huh. I hope not. Else you know what you getting."

"Yes, Mama, corn you corning we," I said meekly.

"Boy, is rude you ruding to me?"

"No, Mama."

Isaac giggled. My mother glared at him and he sidled with his bottom to the door, ready to fly. My mother chose to let it pass so he sat back down. We were eating dinner.

My father muttered under his breath.

"Man planting flowers like blasted sissy. What kind of man plant flowers so like woman?"

At last, on the Saturday morning, we saw him.

When we went up the hill that morning we saw the black Mercedes in the yard. I felt funny. Even Isaac looked almost worried. Hearsay was one thing, but a black Mercedes was another. Everybody knew this was the D Lawrence trademark. This man was serious business for true.

"You 'fraid, Isaac?" I whispered.

"'Fraid? Man, you is idiot?"

And he went boldly into the yard, calling "Hold dog, hold dog!" very loud, just in case the man had a bad dog he would let loose on us. I trailed behind him.

It looked like there wasn't any dog. A man came round the side of the yard. He had a trowel in his hand and he was wearing dirt-stained yard clothes. There was new earth and an earthworm hanging from the trowel. I watched, fascinated, as the worm wriggled and fell off the trowel. The man bent and picked him up and put him to the side like he didn't want to step on him. I jumped like somebody pinched me, realizing I was thinking of the worm like it was a person. It was the way the man held it, all soft and gentle.

He straightened up from putting down the worm and stood looking at us. He didn't look like no black art man. He was a short, red man with a beard and a face that was smiley and sad together. His eyes twinkled. "Hold dog? I not any major kind of dog," he said, looking at Isaac. "Only half dog. The rest of me is man."

"Obeah man?" Isaac shot back, sharp as stone flying from catapult. I tell you, my brother is something else.

"So they say," the man said, chuckling. He had a high-pitched chuckle. "What you think?"

"I don't think you no obeah man," Isaac say boldly. "I think you just a strange stranger."

The man laughed, full and loud this time. "So you not 'fraid of me, then?"

"For what?" Isaac said scornfully.

"And you, little twin?" the man said, looking at me. He had funny, soft eyes, and he looked straight at you when he was talking.

"I not 'fraid neither," I said, feeling glad I had Isaac.

"Well then, since you not 'fraid, you can come and help me do some weeding round the back and then I show you inside my Bluebeard's castle where I tie up little children," he said, laughing again.

We followed him to the back of the house.

It was the weirdest afternoon I ever spent, and the best. He was planting out a new garden in the back and we helped him lay the beds. I planted an orange tree and Isaac planted a pear. He named our trees Isaac and Ishmael, and said we could come and water them any time we wanted, and see how they were doing. He had turtles, real live ones, in a big copper under the house. He let us feed them. They had yellow bellies and opened their mouths with a little gulp to take the food in. It was fascinating. I had never seen turtles before, except sea ones and in books.

His name was Mr Coote. He came from Barbican St Andrew and he used to work in the bank. But he wouldn't tell us why he didn't any more or why he came to Baltree. "A man needs a rest sometimes, lad," was all he said when we asked, and even Isaac shut up.

Afterwards we went inside his house and had lemonade made with Seville orange from Cappi John's tree and brown sugar. It was great, with lots of crush ice from an icebox he kept in a corner of the front room. We made it ourselves, but I was scared. Suppose he had laced the oranges while they were on the tree? Or put something in the sugar when we weren't looking? So at first I didn't want to drink but Isaac stared at me and drank, so I did too.

Inside his house was different from when Cappi John had it. Cappi John had just a bed and makeshift table and chair and jackass-rope tobacco and a donkey hamper thrown down in the corner. Because of the tobacco, the whole house stank.

Mr Coote had the flooring all shined up like a woman. He had this icebox, no fridge, real nice plaited chairs and strange-looking pictures on the wall and some carvings like they come out of deepest Africa. He had a rough chair and table too but they were nice, like somebody made them rough on purpose, not because he couldn't do any better because he was poor.

He saw me looking at one of the pictures, a big one with some people walking in a field with some little red flowers dotted all over it. It looked like somebody had taken a bottle of light the way my mother takes cooking oil, and poured it all over, and it seeped through till the picture was all shining. I couldn't take my eyes off it. "That's a print of a painting by a famous artist named Mon-ay," he said. "M-o-n-e-t, Mon-ay. It's called *Poppies*. Those red flowers are poppies."

"Oh," I said. Until he spelt it, I had thought the famous artist's name was money, but pronounced in a fancy way, like foreign. And I didn't know poppies grew in fields. Girl Guides sold them to raise money for war veterans. They were made of red paper and had black buttons for eyes.

"So why Baltree people don't like you, sir?" Isaac nagged.

Mr Coote chuckled his high chuckle. Then he laughed his loud laugh and said, "You don't know? You don't hear the people say I am a black art man?"

"You cut out people heart and eat them?"

I choked on my lemonade. I didn't know whether to take him seriously or not.

"Damn stupidness," Isaac said, swearing because our mother wasn't there to corn him. "I don't believe a word of it."

"Don't swear, young man," Mr Coote said sternly, not at all like Cappi John. He sounded like he meant it. Isaac looked shamed. "Sorry," he mumbled, ducking his head.

Mr Coote left it at that. He didn't seem to be a man who follow-follow things.

He stared into his lemonade glass, spinning it round and round in his hands, looking sad. After a while he said, like he was talking to himself, "And maybe I am a bad man after all. After all." He sounded very very sad.

"Says who?" Isaac sounded fierce and hot. Isaac was always hot when he liked somebody or something real bad and people were talking silly about it.

Mr Coote didn't seem like he heard him. "Who ever knows himself fully, after all? God alone."

I got scared again so I said, "Mr Coote, you ever been any place besides town and Baltree?"

That changed the subject all right. Mr Coote had been all over the world, London and Bangkok and Paris for real and even a place called Papua New Guinea, which he showed us on a map he fetched from his bedroom.

The afternoon went like lightning. We sat there for hours, listening to Mr Coote tell us about his travels, things like out of books that made my eyes grow out on stalks. I just sat there. I could have listened all night. I was afraid to move to spoil the magic. Isaac asked all the questions.

When Mr Coote looked at his watch and said it was time for small boys to go home, he had changed for ever in my eyes. He was both the nicest ordinariest man in the world and a hero. I felt grateful and happy because it was like God had given us back Cappi John with extras.

"Wait till I tell Newt all those stories about Bangkok," I boasted to Isaac when we were running outside. "Just wait."

Isaac looked at me out of his eyecorner and I knew I had better not tell anybody anything if I knew what was good for me. Mr Coote's stories were to be our secret. That's why I don't put them in this story I telling you now.

That night Uncle Tir, Miss Nellie and several other old people in Baltree came to our yard and whispered with our parents for a long time. They drank tea and rum. We were scared. We knew they had found out about us and Mr Coote. Huddled in our bed, every now and then we could hear a voice raised under the window.

"...Can't stay here, corrupting the little boys."

"...Where he wife? Where he children? Where he people? Where he come from?"

"Inveigling children. He give them any sweetie?"

And my father hissing his teeth. "Chuups. Man

planting flowers like woman. Chuups."

"Send DC. DC wi' know how to handle him."

That was serious. DC was short for District Constable George Washington Sproute. He was called in only in major disputes, like moving people's boundary stones. He was supposed to talk to people friendly like, so they would see reason and behave themselves if they were in the wrong.

Nobody said anything to us that night but the next day we saw DC Sproute pushing the gate to Mr Coote's house and calling out "Hold dog, hold dog!" in his special policeman voice, though he must have known there was no dog there. He just wanted Mr Coote to know he was coming and he was somebody important. Mr Coote came round the side of the house in his yard clothes with his trowel in his hand.

"Good morning, sir," he said politely.

"Morning, morning. I come to see you about a matter, sir," DC Sproute said, just as polite. He felt us staring and turned around and stared at us and then down the road. We went. Mr Coote didn't look at us. I wanted to cry. I wondered if Mr Coote had any worms on his trowel and if they would fall off on DC Sproute. It would serve him right.

When we came home from school on Monday, Mr Coote's house was silent. The black Mercedes was gone and when we knocked no one answered.

"He gone," Newt said, coming up the hill. "Mammy say he make six trips carrying him furniture in him car. He gone."

Isaac stared at Newt like he was mad. He grabbed Newt's father's machete that Newt was carrying. Then he fell on the house in a fury. He hacked at the planks till two of them splintered. He flung away the machete and finished the planks with his bare hands and then he grabbed my hand and we crawled in with Newton behind. Isaac's hands were bleeding. The planks were tougher than when the house was Cappi John's. My hands got sticky with my brother's blood.

Inside there was no sign of Mr Coote or his belongings. The strange pictures and the carvings from deepest Africa were all gone. Everything was bare.

After about a week the grass started to grow up again and the goats started coming. Soon the gorgeous garden would disappear.

Isaac searched for days for a note Mr Coote might have left us, but there wasn't any. Isaac raged. He accused my mother of running him away. My mother lashed him for ruding to her but Isaac didn't care.

"It doesn't make sense!" Isaac cried. "You let us play with Cappi John and he lived alone and he was weird too!"

"That's different," my mother said. "Cappi was one of us. He grow up with us here."

"Mr Coote was a thousand times better than all of you!" Isaac cried. "Better! And don't think it was because he was scared that he went. He wasn't scared! He was just tired of the whole of you, tired of you!"

And he rushed out of the yard and didn't come home till nightdark. I was worried sick and couldn't eat my dinner.

But afterwards he came home. He never said anything after that. For days I felt very lonely, like

I had lost my brother. But one day when we were fishing at Blue Hole without a line the way Cappi John taught us, he suddenly said, "I never want to be a grownup. Never."

His voice sounded hard and bitter. I knew he was thinking about how they treated Mr Coote. I thought it wasn't right either, but I was only a boy and I didn't know what to do. I didn't know how not to be a grownup if God made you grow anyhow, so I just said, "Race you to John Crow Hill."

We raced, and Isaac won.

We never forgot Mr Coote.

Flying With Icarus

Every morning Christorene went down to the beach to watch the waves.

She had lived all her life in a country without sea, and it was all very new and strange. She liked the way the water stretched on and on till it joined the sky, but you couldn't see the end. It made her feel small and almost afraid, but the beach behind and before made her feel safe. She could run up the beach, very fast, her toes digging warm tunnels in the sand that clung like thick, gritty winter socks.

The waves were like people, each had its own personality. The little ones were warm and friendly and only wanted to tickle her toes. The big ones were wild. If she watched long enough, she could count the exact beat on which the big ones came in. They started rolling from far out in the sea's belly, gathering speed and size as they swallowed the little ones in their way.

The big wave curled the sea like a mower. When it got near the beach it heaved mightily, like a giant taking a deep breath. It stood up on its height like feet and vomited water like a living mouth, all over the beach, roaring with triumph and pleasure. It swept far up the beach, sometimes all the way. Sometimes it flung itself so far that it made new patches of beach, sudden bright blazes of sand opening near the mangroves.

Christorene stood in its spray and laughed with terrified joy. The wave washed under her feet and tried to dash her down, but she stood strong, digging her toes deep, letting the wave wet her clothes all over. Seaweed from the wave's vomit hugged her feet like friendly snakes. She flung out her arms and laughed and embraced the wave and the sun. She thought she would die of happiness.

She loved the sea's colours. Sometimes it was blue, blue, blue, just like in the tourist brochures she had seen when she was living in Geneva. But sometimes it was many colours and sometimes it was green and sometimes purple and sometimes many different blues in different places. In the morning it was silver and pink and in the evening silver again and gold, when the sun was setting, shooting long sticks of fire into the water. In rain it was grey, and the rain ran on it like little sticky feet on a wrinkled road. When it was very blue, it had white riders like horses, galloping up and down so softly, softly.

But if you bent far far down and looked directly into the water, it was no colour at all, except some-times a very faint tinge of green, almost invisible. It looked like ordinary water.

Christorene went early early morning before people came, and late evening when people left or were leaving. Then the sea was hers and she could talk to her dad, sending him fast-fast messages through their imaginary conch shell.

"I'm OK, Dad, honest," she told him, watching

the water turn gold under the red and orange blaze of sunset. "I'm getting better. Don't fret." She threw a mollusc shell defiantly into the water. "And I don't care what the others want to do, it's me coming to live with you after the divorce. It's you I'm living with."

And she felt him hugging her, warmly.

But one morning the sea wasn't hers any more. A tall girl about her age was there, throwing sticks into the water. She wore cut-off jeans and a man's shirt with the tails tied above her bare navel. Her hair was a riot of black twists.

"Hi," the tall girl said. "You is Miss Buckeridge bigshot granddaughter from foreign?"

Christorene wanted to say, "I'm not a bigshot," but she felt embarrassed. So she just stood, wondering why the tall girl's face looked odd.

"Shark bite it off," the tall girl said nonchalantly, catching Christorene's stare, and Christorene suddenly realized that the girl's face looked odd because one of her ears was missing.

She blushed, shamed to be caught staring. But her mind, fascinated, imagined the tall girl embroiled in wild, wonderful adventures battling monsters at sea. The girl held out her hand and said, "Charlotte Miller. I live over there." She pointed to the row of tiny houses lining the beachfront.

"Christorene Wray." Christorene shook hands shyly.

Silence fell. Charlotte Miller was unabashedly sizing up Christorene, her eyes bright and inquisitive.

Feeling awkward, Christorene rushed into speech.

"Why are there no seagulls on this beach? I thought every sea had gulls."

"It have gulls but they don't come by where people are," Charlotte said. "They 'fraid people – too much noise. If you want to see seagull you have to go way over the cliff, over there." She pointed towards the bluff that rode the water half a mile away. "I could show you, if you want."

"Now?"

"Why not?"

Christorene stared. Then, "All right," she said, stunned and excited together.

The tall girl led the way westwards until there was no more beach and their bare feet made a road through the water. When they came to the gravelly base of the bluff they started to climb, clutching grass and sharp outcrops to catch a firm hold, not speaking except for occasional grunting instructions from the tall girl whenever Christorene slipped.

They reached the top as the sun rose, and Christorene looked down the other side and cried out.

Now she understood why gulls never came to the people's beach. The people's beach was tame. But here the sea was rough and wild, the spray leaping up like dolphins and hitting against the caverns of the rock below. Christorene could hear the hollow, musical sound it made as it crashed against the rock. It echoed like strange animals singing. Overhead the sky was very high, higher than any sky she had ever seen, huge white clouds wheeling fast across the blue.

There were seagulls everywhere. They wheeled and dived across space, looking sometimes like bits of white paper somebody had half burnt before releasing them into the air, sometimes like a myriad paper kites, and then again, depending on where the sun caught their wings, like pure silk and silver. Their weird cry, *Preewree! Preewree!*, mingled with the crashing waves.

Going down that side was much easier than coming up the other. In minutes the girls stood on the wild beach, watching the gulls torpedo straight and swift and accurate into the water, nine times out of ten coming up with a wriggling fish in their beaks. They didn't pay Charlotte and Christorene any mind.

"People don't come over here, so they not 'fraid," Charlotte said. "Only me-one come. They use to me."

Christorene wasn't listening. She was running towards a white flutter on the beach. "Charlotte, look! I think it's injured!"

Charlotte raced behind her.

It was a very young seagull. It lay half on its side, its upper wing fluttering feebly. Its feathers were matted with sand where it had struggled to move and couldn't. Its eyes were closed but the girls could see its heart beating wild in its chest.

"It's broken," Christorene cried. "Its wing's broken."

Charlotte bent to look. "It going die," she said.

"No!" Christorene cried fiercely. "It can't die, I won't let it."

Charlotte shrugged. "Boy, I don't know what you go do. Any time wild thing injure, it dead. The others not going to look after it — matter of fact they might even kill it — and it can't move to feed itself. And it won't live if you handle it, 'cause it wild. Is so my uncle say."

"We go have to try. We go have to try. Maybe your uncle is wrong. Like doctors are wrong sometimes."

Charlotte stood helpless and puzzled. She couldn't understand this passion. But when Christorene wrapped the little broken thing in her T-shirt and started towards home, she followed, gathering the seaweed Christorene wanted for a hospital nest. And back at Grandma Pearlina's, her efforts were equal to Christorene's.

Christorene's first thought was to find a vet, but Grandma Pearlina opened her eyes wide. "Vet for wild thing? You crazy, child?"

Anyway, the nearest vet was miles away, and Grandma Pearlina said it would be very expensive to get there and also to pay the fee. Even if she could afford it, the seagull would probably die before they arrived.

"We've just got to try then," Christorene cried, fierce and weeping. She dug deep in her mind to remember stuff she had downloaded from the Internet for Milt when he did his project on birds. Together the girls splinted the wing with emery boards held down with masking tape and gauze. They spread the seaweed and then a towel in the bottom of a cardboard box. They punched airholes in the sides of the box so the bird could breathe when they closed the top. Grandma Pearlina lent them a hot water bottle to keep the nest warm.

When they put the seagull in, he lay quietly, only his heart beating so wildly that it set him all atremble. Christorene knew it was because he sensed himself in strange hands and was afraid.

"Don't be scared, little bird," she whispered, putting her mouth close to his head. "Please don't be scared." Her breath fluttered his feathers and his eyelids jumped, but at first they didn't open.

Trying to feed him was more tricky. They tried to prise his beak open with their fingers and feed him some of Grandma Pearlina's Saturday soup, but the beak wouldn't open, and they stopped, scared they might do it damage. Grandma Pearlina watched, not saying anything, but you could tell she thought the seagull would die.

Christorene touched the bird and felt its little warm body and its heart beating faint and fainter. It was like a baby that was going to die before it was born.

"Don't die, little bird, don't die," she willed it fiercely, loving it with all her heart. Through the imaginary conch shell she sent messages to her dad. "Help me, Dad. Don't let it die."

"Don't handle it too much," Grandma Pearlina warned. 'Touch up touch up wild thing too much, it die. Wild thing don't like tame hand."

So Christorene waved her hands low over the

bird instead, fanning love to it through her fingertips.

Charlotte left to do her chores, but Christorene would not leave her vigil by the seagull's bed. She crouched there, frozen, praying.

For a long time the seagull seemed to hover on a bare thread of life. Sometimes the little heart skipped and stopped, struggled raggedly, as if beating its last. And still Christorene held her breath, crying out silently to her dad.

At last, in the warmth of the nest, the heartbeat steadied out, the trembling quieted, and the bird shifted and turned its head. It turned towards Christorene, almost like it could see her. Christorene held her breath. The bruised eyelids opened and the seagull looked directly into her face.

Even Grandma Pearlina got excited when that happened.

"But Jesus God, look how the child magic back the wild thing to life. But girlchild you see, Ah tell you you is a God-bless child, your hand bless the poor bird-soul."

"Thank you, Dad," Christorene whispered into the conch shell.

The seagull relaxed in the nest, as if it had shed a great burden.

The girls were becoming friends. The seagull was getting better. They fed him soup, bread soaked in warm water, and fish. Soon he was flapping his free wing and opening his mouth when they came near.

"He thinks we brought food," Christorene said, giggling. "Greedy thing."

Not only greedy, but fierce! It had become a sort of giggly game, avoiding the sharp jabs from his beak. But he seemed to like when Christorene was near. Only she could feed him without being pecked.

Charlotte carefully touched the head where the feathers had moulted from sickness but were now growing back. "It really picking up. Soon can let it go."

Christorene moved in front jealously, so Charlotte had to let go. She didn't want Charlotte to touch her seagull, even though Charlotte was her friend. She had found and saved him, it was her faith that had woken him, he was hers.

"Soon, little bird, soon," she whispered. "You'll be all right. And me and Dad."

The seagull looked up at her with bright intelligent eyes, cocking his head to one side as if specially listening to what she had to say.

"We have to give it a name," Charlotte said.

"He," Christorene said jealously. "Is a he, not an it. I go call him Icarus 2."

"Icarus 2? What kind of name is that? Call the bird Sinting or Birdielou or some real birdname like that."

"Icarus," Christorene said. "He was a man who wanted to fly, but he fly too near the sun and burn off his wing. This bird go fly again, right out the window and back to where he came from. You go see. That's why he is Icarus 2. He different from the man-Icarus."

She didn't tell Charlotte that Icarus was her father's favourite story character. Or that Icarus 2 was getting better because of her father healing him through the conch shell. All the way from Geneva in Switzerland. Even though Icarus 2 was here in Antigua, in the Caribbean.

83

*   *   *

She had been ill in Geneva. She got colds all the time and finally she got pneumonia and almost died. The doctors said it was stress from her parents' impending divorce. It affected the boys too. Arthur fought at school and Milt stayed in his room all the time with his computer and video games.

Then her grandmother phoned from Antigua in a great anger to her father. "You don't see the child need sunshine and warm? She don't make to live in them kinda cold-cold foreign weather. I did tell you from the child born, this one go different. She a Caribbean child. She ain't go be surviving that gallivanting you be gallivanting from pole to pole in this world, she go need to stay by the sun and the sea. Send the child home to me 'fore God vex with you and tek her."

In the end Mum and Dad decided to send them all away until the divorce came through. Milt and Arthur to Mum's parents in Berne, Christorene to Grandma Pearlina.

She was sad to leave her family and especially

her dad. Even Milt and Arthur, with whom she fought and quarrelled. Her brothers cried when she was leaving and said they would write every day.

"So you can remember Switzerland," Milt said. "Especially at Christmas. I'll send you photos of us in the snow. They don't have white Christmases in the Caribbean."

"No, only sun and sun and coconut trees," Arthur said facetiously. Arthur wasn't impressed with Dad's stories of wonderful life in the Caribbean, and he thought the tourist advertisements he had seen were silly.

Milt kicked his shin. "Idiot." He said to Christorene, "Bring back some of that callaloo and souse Dad is always talking about. Remember anything can travel in the diplomatic bag. You could even bring me a live crab from the sea, nobody would know."

"It would crawl about in the bag and everybody would see," Arthur said scornfully.

"Not if you drugged it first," Milt said. "You could drug its food. I wonder what crabs eat." And

85

his eyes got that faraway look that told you he had gone somewhere else in his mind. Somewhere in the world of crustaceans, and in no time at all he would be on the Internet looking up crab food.

"So how are you going to keep it from stifling, idiot?"

"Easy. It won't be smelling your smelly shoes so it will breathe free."

Arthur lunged at Milt, and the two boys rolled, good-naturedly pummelling each other, on the lawn where they were standing waiting for the airport car. Everyone was glad for the distraction because it made them not feel so sad, although Mum said half-heartedly, "Boys, boys, stop that. That's no way to say goodbye to your sister."

Christorene knew Milt was wrestling with Arthur because he didn't want her to see him crying. Milt was a softie though he pretended otherwise, watching all those kung fu movies and playing Superman video games.

Christorene's mum hugged her and cried a little. "Be well," she whispered, "and bring us back some Caribbean sunshine."

"I will," Christorene said.

"Everything is going to be all right," Mum said. "I promise."

Will it, will it? Christorene cried inside. *How can it ever be all right when you're leaving my dad? You promised him, but you didn't stay. I don't want you to promise me anything!*

But outside she just smiled and hugged Mum.

She didn't cry until it came time to tell Daddy goodbye at the check-in counter. Her dad just held her close for a long time and didn't say anything and Christorene didn't say anything either, but she felt wetness on her cheeks and when he finally let her go she saw they were both crying and she didn't know whose tears were on her face.

"Going to miss you, kiddo," he said, smiling, chucking her under the chin in that way he had, before letting the flight attendant take her.

All the way on the plane, all she could see was her family standing at the last barrier waving au revoir you'll come back soon. But especially her dad with the bright tears in his eyes. She had always been her father's favourite. People said it was because she was delicate and the only girl, but Christorene knew it was more than that. They had a special bond, she and her dad, because they were two of a kind.

I guess it's because we're both shy, Christorene thought to herself, sitting in her window seat watching the cloud-mountains the plane was passing. People don't know Dad's shy, because he's a diplomat, but I do. And then we like the same things, books and art and things like that, and we laugh at the same jokes.

Sometimes when something funny happened, she would catch her dad's eye and he would catch hers, and they'd start laughing at the same time, and Mum and the boys would say "What is wrong with that mad duo again?" "That mad duo" was Mum's nickname for her and Dad. Christorene knew her mum didn't understand her dad. She can't even laugh at his jokes, she thought. Maybe they don't get on because they can't laugh together.

Sometimes it seemed to Christorene that her mum and dad didn't have a thing in common. Milt and Arthur took after Mum. Christorene was the only one of the children who understood Dad's Caribbean things. Or listened to his stories about Antigua, which he called "the lost island of the saints". Life in Antigua didn't sound saint-like, it sounded hard. When her dad was growing up, Grandma Pearlina was very very poor and they could barely survive. But it sounded like life was nice too. Children caught crabs on the beaches and played moonshine baby in the yard on moonlight nights. Grandma Pearlina told them duppy stories on dark nights so they squealed and wouldn't go to the shop after dark.

And the people talked sweet, the way Dad taught her.

Mum was English and had never experienced that life, though she had been for short holidays before the children were born. Milt and Arthur thought it all sounded like a weird dream. Milt and Arthur were thorough Europeans, Dad said, rolling his eyes and rolling out the "o" in "Europeans" in an exaggerated way, so it sounded like "You-*rope*-ians".

"And you're an anachronism, Dad," Arthur mocked, showing off his vocabulary. "A throwback to ancient times. I bet the Caribbean you envisage doesn't even exist any more." Arthur was bright with languages. All the children spoke French and English fluently, but Arthur had a formidable vocabulary and, when he wanted, used words like poetry.

Christorene, though, spoke three languages. She soaked up all the Creole her dad could teach her, so that by the time she was six they were having long conversations in a language only the two of them could fully understand. "Twin. We a twin." She realized she had spoken aloud when the man in the seat beside her said, "You're a twin, little girl?"

I'm not little! Christorene retorted in her mind – but she was a diplomat's daughter and very polite. "Yes," she told the man, and hugged tight the knowledge of this bond between her and her father. She wanted to go to Antigua, to see the Caribbean, but she wished her father could have come too.

"I'll love it for both of us, Dad," she whispered, closing her mind's eye tight tight and concentrating so the message would reach him on wings. It was a trick between them, and in the evenings when he came home she used to ask, "You get the message I send for you today, Dad?"

"Where you send it through?" He'd cuff her ear affectionately. "The conch shell machine?"

"No, the telegram time machine."

"Ah-oh. That is why me never get it. The telegraph system jam-up jam-up bad today, man. You shoulda did blow the conch shell so me coulda hear. You don't know how to take short cut?"

Remembering, Christorene prayed, *Please, God, send him this one through the conch shell so he get it for real.* And she squeezed her hands tight, willing God to answer yes.

Grandma Pearlina met her at the airport, laughing and crying and hugging her in a way that felt of Dad. "Lord have mercy, Lord have mercy, look me dou-dou granddaughter," Grandma Pearlina said, smelling of peppermint and warm. "Girlchild, I woulda recognize you anywhere. You is the spitting image of you father."

Christorene loved her, fiercely and immediately, just for saying that. And then she loved her more, because when Grandma Pearlina stood her back and looked at her, Christorene saw that Grandma resembled Dad too, just like in her photographs.

Many things in Antigua were different from how Dad said, but some were just the way he described. There were so many things that were familiar, it was like they were inside her in pictures and feelings and sounds and smells Daddy had gifted her with from his stories.

Maybe Grandma Pearlina was right, Christorene thought. I'm the one who's Caribbean. I love this place. I wish Dad was here. I wish we could all be a family again, here.

She didn't think Milt would like it, but funny enough, she thought Arthur might. Arthur liked loud, bright things. Antigua was both bright and loud. Everything was in technicolour, like a glorious movie. Trees and grass and people's clothes, everything. When she came off the plane, the bright jewel colours hurt her eyes. There was music in the streets and people talking loudly and gesticulating.

At first Christorene thought they were quarrelling, and she was scared. But Grandma

Pearlina laughed. "Quarrel? No sah, them nah quarrel, them just a-discuss. Some a dem a-greet." She hissed her teeth, chuups, like Dad when he was mocking or fed up. "And some a dem just a-talk people business. Anyone you hear mekking the most noise, people business dem a-mind, 'stead a minding fe-dem own."

Grandma Pearlina took her round and showed her off to the neighbours.

"Me granddaughter from Switzerland. Is the one and only girlchild for me son. Pretty eh?"

"Pretty like money," people agreed, speaking in their lilting, up-and-down voices. "The mother white, nuh?"

"She pretty from her father side," Grandma Pearlina retorted, tossing her black head proudly. "Is me the looks come from."

"Is true, is true for true. So she come to live with you now, Miss Buckeridge?"

"No sah, she jus' a-spend holiday," Grandma Pearlina said. She told Christorene not to tell anybody her parents were divorcing. "These people too inquisitive."

Christorene went to the market with Grandma Pearlina. She loved the bright mounds of fruit and food, heaped glowing on the ground and on the stalls. And it was hilarious when Grandma Pearlina haggled with the vendors, accusing them of cheating her.

"Ooman, you think I plant money-tree in me backyard for me and you? What kind of tourist price them there you telling me?"

"Tourist price is double that," the vendor retorted. "I drop the price for you becausen I see you is a ole ooman and don't have nobody to mind you."

"Mind me? Mind me? Ooman, you see me come in here looking for charity? But you out of order. Sell me the split peas mek I go me ways. And I not paying more than fifty cents a pound neither." She paid fifty cents a pound. The vendor sold her, still cussing good-naturedly.

Christorene didn't like the crazy drivers on the road and sometimes she didn't like the heat, although mostly the sun was nice. When she closed her eyes it was red against her eyelids.

In Switzerland it was orange. It seemed to her that people were richer than when Dad was a boy, but they weren't always so nice. They stared at her and laughed when she spoke Creole in her English-French Swiss accent.

"But is where you come from?" some people jeered, so that Christorene stopped speaking in public.

Only the sea was perfect. Christorene had seen sea in Europe, but not like this. This was her father's sea, and it was the most beautiful sea in the world. The first time she saw it, she cried. And now she knew the sea loved her, because it had sent her Icarus.

Charlotte made up a story about Icarus. Charlotte was always making up stories about things. Like the one about the shark biting off her ear. Grandma Pearlina said it wasn't true, Charlotte lost her ear in a motor accident. In Charlotte's story, Icarus had come over many seas from Switzerland where Christorene lived. "He come to look for you with a message from your family because he know they missing you," she said. "But duppy jealous you and hit him *wham!* – and break he wing. But still he fly till he reach near the place where you living but he couldn't fly any further so he dropdown on Brydson Bay. And see, God tell you where he be and that's how you find him."

Christorene thought Charlotte's story wasn't so bad, except it wasn't what really happened. What happened was, her dad sent her strength through the conch shell so she could give it to Icarus so he would get well. Dad sensed everything that was happening with her and he knew that if Icarus died she would be sad.

Every evening at six on the dot, Dad rang her from Switzerland. Sometimes he sounded far away because there was static on the phone, sometimes he sounded near. She told him about Charlotte and the gulls and the market and the beach, and eating souse and callaloo and being afraid of the people at first and the crazy driving cars. But she didn't tell him about Icarus. Somehow, she felt if she told him it would spoil their secret communication through their imaginary conch shell. She wanted him to feel

the vibes through their shell and know her secret
without telling. Then she'd know they were still all
right, she and Dad, they would never split up even
though the family was splitting up.

"Something bothering you, sugarplum?" he said
one evening after she found Icarus. "I feel some
vibes that you not telling me."

"Check the conch shell, Daddy," she said,
feeling glad.

"OK, kiddo, I will."

Icarus was trying to fly. He fluttered out of his
nest, struggling towards the window. Every day for a
while Christorene moved him out of the dark where
he was healing and put him near the window so he
could see outside and know he was not caged. That
he was free.

But his injured wing was still too weak and
after several tries he fell back in the nest.

"Soon, little bird, very soon now," Christorene
whispered, stroking at his head but not touching
him in case he still died, like Grandma said.

Icarus looked at her with his bright dark eyes.

Preewree! Preewree! he said. Christorene cried out in delight, because she knew he was answering her back.

It took him three weeks to heal. On the day he flew, Christorene was by Charlotte's, helping her cut up coconut to cook rice and peas. When she got home, late, Icarus wasn't there.

"Grandma," Christorene cried. "The seagull gone! Is you open the window mek cat eat him?"

"I open the window," Grandma Pearlina said serenely, "but no cat don't eat him. I in the kitchen and I hear a noise and when I go to look, is the bird there on the sill, fluttering and begging to get out. So Ah let him out."

"He flew, Grandma, he flew?"

"Oh yes, girlchild, he fly. Raise up off that sill and into that air like God-self put a hand under him and sail him on pure soul. You shoulda see how him tek that wind and rise."

Christorene ran to the window, straining to see if she could see her beloved seagull. But of course she couldn't. He was gone. She remembered a line from a poem Dad read to her: "And they are gone:

aye, ages long ago these lovers fled away into the storm."

She and Charlotte went down the other side many times to watch the gulls wheeling and crying in the thin, pure air and the golden sunshine. They tried hard to see if they could spot Icarus, and once Charlotte said, "See him there!", pointing to a small gull with brown on its white wings like Icarus. But Christorene wasn't sure.

She cried a little but in the end it was all right. "Sometimes things don't come back," Dad used to say. "But it's all right, because they still stay with you, here," he said, touching his heart. "So long as you love them."

That evening Dad phoned and said the custody had been decided and she was to live with him. The boys would stay with Mum but they would swap around in the holidays.

Christorene was silent with joy. She had been so scared that because she was a girl they would send her with Mum.

"Are you there, sugar?" Dad said anxiously.

"Yes, Daddy, I'm fine."

"I getting a vibe," Dad said. "I sense you kinda happy, something good happen to you today."

"Yes, Dad," Christorene said. "Oh yes!"

And in her mind she said, *Thank you, Icarus. Thank you, sea.*

She knew Icarus was a sign. She and Dad would have sadness but they were going to be all right. And when they came back here together she would take him down the bluff to Brydson Bay and show him where seagulls still lived, wheeling in the sunshine.

Miss Mandy
and the
Lost Girl

Miss Mandy is down by the guinep tree talking to Zachary again.

Zachary is her son, who was taken in a plane crash in South America, and Miss Mandy can't stop grieving. No body came home, her son is dead and not dead. Oh Miss Mandy, Miss Mandy has to be mourning and not mourning. In the end she's taken away to the hospital. Now she's back she's all right, but she still talks to Zachary. Every morning, every evening, like prayers, Miss Mandy is by the guinep tree, calling her son, her son, her son.

"Mandy mind gone, gone," people say, shaking

their heads. "Poor lady. And was the one son."

"Miss Mandy mad now, Sister?" Aldo wants to know, looking out the window to where Miss Mandy mourns among the guinep leaves.

"Not mad, little brother, not mad. Just grieving."

"So her mind will come back soon?"

"Soon, little brother, soon."

"When all the grief leak out and her head done wash out," Hickory says, nodding wisely.

He falls silent, thinking of Miss Mandy's grief like a bucket with a hole in the end.

"The lost girl following Miss Mandy again," he says suddenly, craning his neck and kneeling up on the window seat to see better.

Aldo scrambles up beside his cousin, scrunching him to one side so he too can see better.

Sister shakes her head and goes into the kitchen to finish cooking dinner. She does not want another long argument about who is madder, Miss Mandy or the lost girl. With Aldo and Hickory, it could take the whole day. Especially Hickory. Not even digging for worms and beetles in the backyard is as interesting to Hickory as Miss Mandy and the lost girl.

The lost girl climbs up on the fence to watch Miss Mandy greeting her dead again. Miss Mandy's dress passing brushes the lost girl's leg, but she does not see. Her eyes are over and far away, like Tom Tom the Piper's son, the lost girl thinks to herself. The lost girl thinks that Miss Mandy looks like she has been taken too. And she feels oh, so sad for Miss Mandy. She wishes she could hug Miss Mandy and tell her how sad she is for her that her son died. But though she opens her mouth she has no sound, no sound.

"Why the lost girl cannot speak, Sister?" Hickory calls to Sister in the kitchen. He asks this question every day. "Her tongue cut out? If she open her mouth wide wide, you wouldn't see any tongue?"

"She has a tongue, Hickory," Sister says patiently. "But she cannot speak. Some people born like that. They just cannot speak."

"They just dumb, dumb-dumb," Aldo says

grandly, showing off his knowledge. "Right, Sister?"

"Right, but don't call your cousin dumb-dumb. Where you learn that language from?"

Aldo says sorry, but behind Sister's back he makes an unrepentant face at his cousin. Hickory ignores him, tickling a moth that has landed on the windowsill and contemplating the mystery of the lost girl. "I go grab her and open her mouth and look in there. One day..." he promises, putting his arms on the windowsill and his chin on his arms and watching the lost girl watching Miss Mandy calling the dead. He has forgotten the moth, which staggers secretly away.

"Your dinner on the stove, Zachy," Miss Mandy whispers to the leaves. "Hot and ready for when you come home. Rice and peas and Sunday chicken just as how you like it."

The wind whispers in the guinep leaves. *Yes, Mama*, the wind answers.

"Try and come home by six o'clock," Miss Mandy says. "Rain set up, might fall."

The wind murmurs, *Yes, Mama, yes.*

The lost girl on the fence is within a hand's touch but Miss Mandy does not see. The hem of Miss Mandy's dress floats in the little scurries of breeze and touches the lost girl's feet. In her heart the lost girl weeps. Poor poor Miss Mandy, the lost girl says in her heart. He won't eat the rice and peas, Miss Mandy. The dead only want rum and white rice. You have to pour it in the ground for him to take.

Miss Mandy cannot hear what is in the lost girl's heart. She goes on whispering to the dead, her lips moving like half asleep. But still the lost girl hears all her words, softer than falling leaves.

The lost girl cannot bear the pain. She slips down from her seat on the fence and tugs Miss Mandy's hem, oh so softly, so softly.

Miss Mandy turns around and looks through the lost girl like looking through water. "Shi fly, shi." She swats at the lost girl thinking she is a fly. "Get off me dress hem."

And she goes down the darkening road, still talking softly to the dead. The lost girl follows her, still holding Miss Mandy's hem. Miss Mandy still swats at the fly humbugging her legs, but the lost girl does not let go. Every day she has followed the lady with the unseeing eyes, and now her heart is breaking, breaking.

Miss Mandy reaches her wire-fence gate. "Hold dog, hold dog!" she calls to her own house, and waits. Nobody comes out but Miss Mandy says, "Thank you, me son. Nice you come open the gate for Mama. And Ah see you reach home before six o'clock." Miss Mandy curtsies and smiles. She pushes her own gate like she is helping another hand to hold it open.

The lost girl lets go the hem and touches Miss Mandy's waist. Miss Mandy jumps, turns, and looks down in surprise. Miss Mandy has seen the lost girl. "Who you?" She looks at the lost girl with suddenly glittering eyes.

The lost girl simply smiles up at Miss Mandy, and Miss Mandy sees the tears in her eyes.

Miss Mandy jerks, like someone hit her shoulder blades. "Who you?" she repeats. "You come from where me son is? You come with message from Zach?"

The lost girl has made Miss Mandy unsure what

is real and what is not. If the lost girl comes with a message, maybe Zach has not come home after all. But if he has not come home, where is he?

The lost girl smiles, shaking her head from side to side. She raises her thin hand and touches Miss Mandy's cheek.

Miss Mandy seizes the lost girl's hand.

"Come in," she tells the lost girl. "Come in and tell me the message he give you. He well? When last you see him, he well?"

The lost girl touches Miss Mandy's other cheek. Her fingers are lighter than leaves. "Oh God," Miss Mandy says. "Me son. Me son."

Miss Mandy fumbles with her door latch, pushes the door open and pulls the lost girl in. As the door closes, the lost girl smiles and touches Miss Mandy's eyes.

"Sister, Sister, come quick, come quick," Hickory cries, dancing up and down in his place on the window seat in great excitement. "Miss Mandy carry the lost girl gone into her house! Miss Mandy carry the lost girl gone into her house!"

Sister hurries from the kitchen, peeling knife in hand. She leans over the boys, staring through the window at Miss Mandy's closed front door. "Lord have mercy," Sister murmurs. "I hope to God she don't do that child anything, in her mad distress. Better go call Miss Pularchie."

"Yes, yes," Aldo agrees enthusiastically, glad of any excuse to go on the road. "I wi' go call her, I wi' go call her," and before Sister can say, "Wait, I don't send you anywhere, I going myself," Aldo is out the door and running. Hickory is after him like a shot.

They race to Miss Pularchie's and blurt out the story breathlessly. "And she hold her dress hem and she follow her till she reach her gate and sudden so Miss Mandy grab her and pull her inside like black art man and sudden so the door shut, BAM!" Hickory slaps his hands together as he says BAM! to give Miss Pularchie the sound of the door bamming.

Miss Pularchie says, "Awright, I wi' go down there and see what happen."

"Ah can come, Mammy, Ah can come?" Miss Pularchie's one dozen children crowd around their mother's skirts, jumping up and down in excitement.

"Come where, come where? Go right back in the house go do what you have to do and don't let me come back and find it not done," Miss Pularchie says sternly. Her husband Mr Marcus comes out of the house and says to the children, "You hear your mother? Find youself back in here right right now."

"But suppose she killing her, Mammy?" wails Marlette, the eldest girl. "You go need us to help you overpower her and save Lost Girl."

Miss Pularchie gives her one look and Marlette retreats, defeated. Aldo and Hickory hurry behind Miss Pularchie but when they reach Miss Mandy's closed door Miss Pularchie turns and says, "Awright, go back up to Sister now," and the two boys have to go, hangdog.

"Maybe Miss Mandy wi' look inna her mouth and pull up her tongue so it come right," Hickory says hopefully, thinking only of the lost girl. His eyes glisten with speculation.

"Lord, how you so fool?" Aldo grabs his arm and hauls him, wriggling and protesting, back up the track towards their yard. But in his vision Hickory the dreamer sees Miss Mandy pull up the lost girl's tongue and hears the lost girl speak.

A strange thing has happened in the district of Peter's Peace. Miss Pularchie is allowing the lost girl to keep company with mad Miss Mandy. How could Miss Pularchie do such a thing, expose a dumb child to a madwoman? What harm might her mad ravings do that the child could not tell in words or save herself from? And suppose Mandy physically harmed the child?

"Pularchie brave," Sister says, half to herself, half to Aldo and Hickory as she gives them their dinner. "I coulda never take such a chance."

"Is because is not her child," other people say. "Not hers so she don't care. I bet she woulda never do that with her own."

Miss Pularchie explains herself, leaning over her fence so the neighbour she's talking to and the neighbours passing can hear. "I think long and thorough 'bout this," Miss Pularchie says, "and I think it for the best. When I push open that door and go in, I see the two of them sitting good good at table, Mandy giving the child good food to eat. And I listening to what going on, and is the first since Zach gone I hear Mandy sound so sane. I hear her explaining to the little child that her son dead and it cause her head to tek her sometimes. Is the first I hear Mandy admit that Zach really dead. The child have some good effect on her, man."

"Yes, is true," Miss Mandy's neighbour murmurs in sympathy. "I never see Mandy so sane since."

"The child. That is what gets me," Miss Pularchie says, wiping a tear from her eye. "From the two of them walking, I see her really making effort to talk. You see the little mouth trembling, trembling and twisting to get the words out to talk to Mandy, though not a thing coming. That's why I know that girl don't born dumb."

"She twist her mouth like this," Marlette cries, listening from the doorway where Miss Pularchie's dozen children are crowded. She makes a hideous clown's face that sets the other children laughing. "But still she can't talk!" Marlette shrieks, bent double with laughter. Miss Pularchie swats absently at her with her apron hem, and Marlette subsides in giggles.

"I think there go be a breakthrough one day soon," Miss Pularchie says stoutly, like she is trying to convince herself. "One day soon. Something in Mandy click with that girl. I believe we go see something happen one day soon. Soon we go hear that lost girl voice."

"Hmm," the neighbour says. "Pularchie, I agree with you." But behind Miss Pularchie's back she tells the next neighbour, "I think the Children's Services people shoulda come and take back that child from Pularchie. For either Pularchie stark staring mad sheself or she just finding excuse to get rid of the child. You know is Mandy feeding her now?"

And it is true. Every day now it is Miss Mandy and the lost girl trekking the fields, Miss Mandy talking in her blue voice to her son, and the lost girl behind her, looking up in Miss Mandy's face and holding tight to her hem. Sometimes her hand steals softly into Miss Mandy's hand, and Miss Mandy does not pull hers away. Sometimes she looks down suddenly at the lost girl as if seeing her for the first time. She starts, frowns, and asks, "Who you?"

The lost girl cannot answer. She smiles.

"You bring message from me son?"

But every day Miss Mandy is becoming more real, learning to accept the truth. "You know me son dead?" she asks suddenly one day, giving the lost girl dinner behind her latched door after they have walked, talking to the leaves. The lost girl nods her head and smiles.

"Dead," Miss Mandy repeats. "Yes, dead. Plane crash, just tumble down out of the sky." And she puts her head down on her arm and weeps.

The lost girl gets up from her chair and hugs Miss Mandy. Miss Mandy hugs her back, tight tight, until Miss Pularchie comes to take the lost girl home.

Miss Mandy begins to talk to the lost girl about her son, like a sane woman. And one day she says sadly, "I not mad, you know. I know you don't come from where he be. I know you don't bring any message from me son. You is just a ordinary, live

113

girl." She looks at the lost girl and shakes her head, so sadly, sadly. "Poor poor motherless," she croons, and hugs the lost girl.

The lost girl hugs Miss Mandy's feet. There are tears in her eyes, and her lips work themselves and struggle to speak.

"I know why Lost Girl can't talk," Aldo tells Hickory triumphantly. "I hear Miss Pularchie say so."

"Liar," Hickory says. Then, eyes bright with expectation, he asks, "Why?"

"Nah tell you. Two dollar first."

"I don't got no two dollar."

"Then you can't hear then."

Hickory gives in. "Awright. I lend you my truck for one whole evening."

"No, two evening."

"One." Hickory is using his truck as a hospital bed for a lizard he's fondled half to death, and he doesn't want the lizard to have no bed for two whole nights.

"Two, take it or leave it."

The boys bargain until Aldo gets his two

evenings. "Don't bother come try to use it when is my time to use it, you know. Ah-oh," he warns.

"Just cool, man, cool," Hickory says. "Tell me the story now."

Aldo settles down to tell the story, a glint in his eyes. "She wasn't born so, is not so it go," he begins, spitting in the road like big man. "She coulda talk and then something bad happen to her and she stop talking and she run away. She run away come here and Miss Pularchie take her in."

Hickory wriggles impatiently. "But what bad happen to her why she can't talk?"

"How I must know?" Aldo retorts, exasperated. "I was there?"

Hickory feels cheated. He has given up his truck two evenings for nothing. He knows the rest of the story. He remembers the late evening the lost girl arrived in the district unable to say who she was or where she was going or where she was coming from. They gave her paper to write and she began to cry instead. Miss Pularchie took her to the police station and the police wanted to keep her in the station lock-up till they put it over the radio and somebody claimed her. But Miss Pularchie was having none of that, so she took the lost girl home and waited for the police to put it over the radio and somebody to come and claim the lost girl. But nobody came.

Miss Pularchie went to the Children's Services people in the town and they said they would search for the lost girl's people. When Miss Pularchie went back many times, the Children's Services people said they had done all they could, but no one had come to claim the lost girl. She was like a parcel that had been lost. "Like somebody leave her on a bus seat," Hickory said, when he heard. "Leave her and forget her, like a parcel."

"Dumb-dumb," Aldo said. "Parcel can get up and walk?"

The Children's Services people said they could either put the lost girl in a home, or Miss Pularchie could keep her. They would pay her to be the lost girl's foster mother.

Miss Pularchie wasn't sending the lost girl to no children's home.

"No sir, no way," Miss Pularchie said. "I hear

too much wicked things they do to people's children in those homes. I wi' keep her. Jesus God know it hard, but I wi' keep her. God wi' help me."

"Is because Pularchie want the government money," people said.

But Miss Pularchie didn't get much money from the government to keep the lost girl. Still she kept her, and the lost girl didn't go any worse than her own children. She was no hungrier and no dirtier than Miss Pularchie's children, who were always hungry and squeaky clean. She went to school with Miss Pularchie's children and the other children teased her because she could not speak. Miss Pularchie quarrelled and punished her own children when they teased the lost girl, but still the children teased. The lost girl only cried. Nobody knew if she learnt anything in class since she never wrote. She only cried.

I guess she follow Miss Mandy because Miss Mandy lonely like her, Hickory thinks to himself, digging in the backyard for worms. From Miss Mandy mad, nobody else keep all-day company with her.

People greeted Miss Mandy howdy-do and saw to it that she had food and looked after herself, but only the lost girl stayed.

And Hickory wonders what happened bad to the lost girl why she cannot speak.

Miss Mandy is better. Everyone says so. She is now calling howdy to her neighbours and doing her farming. The lost girl follows her everywhere. People are glad and start talking happily about Miss Mandy.

"Pularchie better give that child to Mandy," people say. "Look like her company save Mandy life."

One day Hickory and Aldo are at their gate swinging and looking out and lo and behold, Miss Pularchie drives up with a tall man in a white car. The car stops at Miss Mandy's house and Miss Pularchie and the tall man come out. Miss Pularchie is huffing and puffing with excitement.

"Zachary come home," she announces to all of Peter's Peace. "Lord have mercy, Zachary come home! He never dead, he survive the plane crash!

Lord have mercy, he just stop at me gate to ask me where he mother is. Lord have his mercy! Lord have his mercy!" She lifts her apron and wipes her face vigorously. Miss Pularchie is fat and gets hot easily. "Mandy! Mandeee! Mandy-oh!" She lifts her voice mightily, even before she gets breath back.

"Who calling?" Miss Mandy comes round from the back of the house, closely followed by the lost girl. "Oh, is you, Pularchie. What you want?"

"Your child come home!" Miss Pularchie puffs, pointing at the tall man.

A crowd gathers. The tall man walks towards Miss Mandy, arms outstretched. "Mama," he says. "Mama!" His voice is like a strong guitar breaking.

Miss Mandy stands there looking like she has seen a ghost. She cannot move or speak. The tall man reaches her and hugs her close and tight, and Miss Mandy begins to cry, like dying, like dying.

"Zach, is you? Is *you*? You not dead?"

"No, Mama, I am not dead. I've been in a hospital in Buenos Aires all these months. I lost my memory, forgot my name."

119

Someone is weeping, weeping, weeping. Loud and long, and long.

It's the lost girl.

The lost girl's face contorts, huge roots rise in her cheeks, her forehead. Her mouth struggles and convulses. Ropes of anguish stark and stiffen her body, like birthing.

"Sister, Sister!" Hickory is screaming, jumping up and down. "She's talking! Listen, Lost Girl is talking!"

The lost girl is talking, under her sobs. Her words scrape like pipes that are rusted.

"Don't take her away," the lost girl begs the tall man. "Be glad, but don't take her away."

Miss Mandy lets go of the tall man and looks at the lost girl there weeping, weeping. She holds out her arms to the lost girl and clasps her close. "Poor poor motherless," Miss Mandy says, her voice like crooning.

The crowd, muttering and exclaiming before, now blazes into laughter and shouts and prayers and song.

*   *   *

The guinep tree is late blossoming and Aldo and Hickory have each grown two centimetres in the summer. Aldo is showing off his new height to all the world, and racing Hickory's truck. Hickory is busy. He's graduated from beetles and lizards and worms, and is raising a guinea pig named Snout. He's feeding Snout, cleaning Snout's house of wire and wood, strewing fresh grass on Snout's bedroom floor, talking to Snout for hours and hours, and watching Snout's pink nose twitch like a little wet mollusc in a shell.

He likes to tell Snout stories, and the latest news. "Miss Pularchie came yesterday," he tells the guinea pig, watching the pink nose twitch as though it can smell the news.

"She heard from Miss Mandy and the lost girl. They doing well, up there in Kingston. They coming to look for her."

Snout moves up close to Hickory and snuffles wetly at his palm.

"Greedy thing," Hickory scolds, tickling the little pink nose. "You don't want to hear the news? Thursday. They coming Thursday. Miss Mandy and the lost girl and Miss Mandy's son. Miss Mandy is all right."

Snout looks aggrieved. He wants food, not news.

"The lost girl is all right too. Miss Mandy son adopted her. They talk to her people and her people say it's OK and he adopt her. She and Miss Mandy happy happy." Hickory sticks a blade of grass thoughtfully into Snout's nose. The guinea pig twitches and sneezes in disgust.

"The lost girl told them where to find her people. She couldn't talk because her mom and dad burnt in a fire. That's the bad thing that happen to her. She was scared she'd have to go and live with her people, so she runned away. Her people bad people. Miss Pularchie say they sell drugs. They thought she died in the fire. But she just runned away."

Hickory softly pinches the guinea pig's nose just to hear it squeal. Obligingly, Snout squeals. "Pay attention," Hickory commands sternly. Then he tells the guinea pig, "I like living with Sister. Even though she's only my cousin. I wouldn't run away."

He pauses. "She's Aldo's real sister."

Snout is tired of him, so he doesn't answer. Instead, he puts his head down into his chest and pretends to fall asleep.

The boy smiles. He looks up and over the guinea pig's house and his face has gone far away. It is Hickory the dreamer and in his mind he is seeing Miss Mandy with the lost girl, and in his vision he sees Miss Mandy open the lost girl's mouth and pull up her tongue and smooth it out in its right place and at last the lost girl speaks. He knows this is how it happened, that it is so.

"Come let Ah feed you," he says to the guinea pig, and goes to fetch Spanish needle.

DREAD MILDRED

I don't know if you have an aunt like Mildred, but if you haven't, give thanks and behave yourself, because there are some me-e-e-an beings somewhere who dish out relatives. They might send you a Mildred. Boy, if every aunt was like Mildred and you wanted to put a curse on your worst enemy, all you'd have to do is pray "Send him an aunt!" and that would be the end of him.

Shikes! From just the name alone, you know Mildred is dread, dreader than dread. Mildred is our aunt by our mother's side but she isn't anything like the rest of our family. Our six other aunts are rational beings who understand that children must do their own thing sometimes – should be most of the time, if you ask me. Mildred believes in the iron hand of discipline, and she'll sock it to you with an iron smile. Except that Mildred doesn't really smile, she grimaces. Like her face has constipation.

You think I could call Mildred "Mildred" to her face? No, sirree! I gotta be real correct and proper, so when I'm talking to her it has to be Yes, Auntie Mildred, No, Auntie Mildred, Three bags full, Auntie Mildred. It's only because I'm telling you this story I get the chance to say Mildred, but in real life it isn't easy. The woman has remote radar in her headback. She hears things you are thinking before you even do them.

Like, I mean, I'm sitting in my room minding my own business and Mildred comes in and says, "Don't think you can get out of dusting that bookshelf, you know. I want it dusted, and I want it dusted today, today. So don't come telling me at day's end that you forget." I mean, she has been nagging at me all day about dusting this bookshelf by day's end, yet she's made five trips into my room to harass me to go and do it, and it's not day's end yet. I mean, *of course* I'm planning to forget the bookshelf, but that's just because she keeps nagging, nagging like that. And how does she know that's what I'm planning? Jeez!

Or she comes out in the yard and says, "Brenda, where are the socks I told you to wash?" just at the exact minute you're thinking of pushing them down in the garbage bin so you won't have to be forever scrubbing and scrubbing these horrid things that are supposed to be white but always keep forgetting their real colour after PE. Mildred said we had to wash our small things ourselves because one day we mightn't have a washing-machine and then we'd have to do it all by hand. Being Mildred, she had to think of the worst case scenario, just so she could turn you into a slave. Left up to her, my hands would be sore from washing, morning, noon and night.

And she doesn't let go a single thing. Man, if you could have a human bulldog, Mildred would be it. My other aunts will leave you alone so long as you don't injure yourself and cost them money to go to the doctor. With Mildred, you can't breathe, much less *do* anything.

Just to give you an example. One time Miss Atkinson said now we had returned to school after indulging in too much Christmas cake and things, we were to write a composition: "My New Year's Resolution".

I wrote: "My New Year's Resolution is to take charge of my life and make my own decisions. I don't want my aunt making them for me any more."

Well, what do you know? I tell you, the woman has radar eyes. Was like a sixth sense in the back of her head telling her when there was stuff to harass you with. I come home hot and tired from PE and I barely manage to eat my dinner, watch cartoons and pretend to take a shower. Two twos Mildred is calling me into her study and looking at me with grave face.

"Sit down, Brenda," Mildred says, looking at me over the top of her glasses. She can't see anything without her glasses. But people like Aunt Mildred don't need eyes – as I said, she's got radar.

"I like to stand, Aunt Mildred." I want to be on

my feet to handle whatever's coming. I dig my toes into the carpet and brace myself like Horatio at the bridge.

"Suit yourself." Aunt Mildred has this way of sounding sweet, but don't be fooled, it's all a ploy to destabilize you.

"I was sorting through your book bag yesterday," Aunt Mildred says.

Shikes! I had forgotten this woman doesn't believe in privacy. Every weekend she invades our space and looks in our exercise books to see what we're doing in school. If she doesn't like what she sees, she calls you up, asks you a lot of questions, and then either goes to see your class teacher or sends you for extra lessons – or worse yet, teaches you herself. Tell you the truth, Mildred isn't a bad teacher. She can make things really interesting and she knows a lot of stories, like about Horatio at the bridge and Hannibal crossing the Alps with elephants and the Spanish Inquisition where some religious madmen fried people in oil for their beliefs, and what caused the Second World War and all about Hitler and Mussolini and slavery and colonization, and how the Arawaks discovered Columbus and why black people love to travel so.

But she won't ease up until you get everything right. Now I'm a person like this; I don't like to work too much and sweat out myself. The Bible says sweating was a curse on Adam for disobedience, and I don't want no curse following me. So I will work until I feel my brain getting hot, and then I have to take a rest. Mildred got mad one time because she said she noticed if I had a hundred maths for homework, I'd get the first fifty right and the second fifty wrong.

"You do that consistently, so I know it's not inability," Mildred said. "I know it's sheer laziness. Brenda, nothing is wrong if you work till you tired you know. In fact if you not tired you not working."

What kind of crook-up logic is that? Mr Tired don't tell you "go and work", he tell you "go and rest", not so? I never hear anybody say, "I tired so I go work." I hear them say, "I tired so I go rest."

Well, anyways, there is me standing before Aunt Mildred trying desperately to remember how dirty I had left the book bag yesterday. Was it smelling of leftover lunch? Had milk spilt all over the books because I put the leftovers in the book bag instead of the lunchbox because the book bag was easier to reach? I racked my brains but couldn't find a thing. The bag had been clean that morning when I packed it for school, so it couldn't be dirt. So it must be maths again. I had got only seventy-six out of a hundred on the last test. Wasn't it just like Mildred, jumping on you years after she discovered something, like she had to plan strategy how to attack you? Two whole days she waits, and then she makes sure my belly is full and I am well relaxed before she pounces.

"I found something very interesting," Mildred continues. "Your composition entitled 'My New Year's Resolution'."

Shikes! I'd totally forgotten about that. At first I'd left it there deliberately for her to see, just for spite. But then I got a little cold feet, not much, and decided not to leave it lying around after all. But I forgot to put the exercise book in the bottom closet drawer. I hadn't got a good mark anyhow. Miss Atkinson said my composition was too short.

That make sense to you? Don't you supposed to be firm and brief when making a resolution?

"What I want to know" – Mildred is coming in for the kill – "What I want to know is, what decisions you want to make for yourself at your age? And what decisions do I make for you that you should be making for yourself?"

I think rapidly and decide to do a full block. That means you pretend total innocence, like you had nothing to do with this at all and it was really someone else's handwriting, not yours.

"Nothing, Aunt Mildred." I try to sound stupid and surprised at the same time.

"What you mean 'nothing'? That is not an answer. Nothing what?"

"I don't want to make any decisions for myself, Aunt Mildred. And I don't think you making too much decision for me."

"So who write this composition? Not you?" I can hear the impatience creeping into Mildred's voice. I wriggle my big toe in the carpet with glee. She is getting rattled. "Yes, is me, Auntie. But it don't mean anything, is just a composition."

"Is just a composition? Brenda, look here. Cut the hypocrisy. Is me you talking to. You know I know you better than that. So talk straight with me. Do me that courtesy – I have always talked straight with you."

That is true. Straight as a knife that just sharpen and cutting through bread. I shift my ground.

"Well, just *some* decisions. Not all." I bend my head and look at her from my eyecorners, cross-eyed like Aunt Carmen, so she doesn't know I'm really looking at her.

"Like which ones?"

I didn't plan for this, so I have to think.

Mildred doesn't like silence, she's always talking, talking, talking.

"You know, Brenda, I have always tried to be democratic about the decisions made in this house. I make rules, yes, but don't I always explain to you the reason for the rules?"

It's not a rhetorical question. It's a Spanish Inquisition. "Yes, Aunt Mildred."

"So I ever give you any unreasonable rules?"

"No, Aunt Mildred."

"So then which decisions I make that you find unsuitable so you have to make your own?"

Three bags full, Aunt Mildred. Out loud I say, "Bible say man must free. God make man to free." I wanted to spite her, so I was quoting her own words back at her. Plus she was winning the debate and I had to fight back. I couldn't just let her beat me.

"So what is freedom?"

I am really getting mad now. "Auntie, you is Socrates or something? Why you keeping philosophy class over one little composition?"

"Is not one little composition, is a principle. You talking about freedom, but I don't think you understand freedom. Nobody is totally free. I am not totally free. At work, I make decisions, but I also have to obey my boss. Otherwise the whole organization falls apart. In the same way I allow you some freedoms, but there are some rules I make you just have to obey, for your own good. You don't see?"

I button my mouth shut.

"So talk to me. Which decisions you want to

make for yourself? I want to hear. And I promise you, if I think they are reasonable, we can negotiate something."

I hate when she pretends to be reasonable, because you know you can't win. Somewhere up the line she's waiting like a calaban, ready to trip you up and do you in.

"Well, for example, I don't see why you should force me to eat vegetables." I say the first thing that comes into my head, making my voice sound really bitter.

Aunt Mildred goes into her usual sermon about vegetables, vitamins and minerals and keeping healthy and having pretty skin and all that jazz. Why can't she be like real parents and guardians and just cook the food nice and let you eat it without knowing it's got vegetables in? And why she has to preach sermon about everything she go do? Why she don't just do it? I tune her out and wait for the conclusion. Finally she says, "OK, let's make a compromise."

The compromise is I'm to eat only vegetables I like, since I have to eat vegetables anyway. When she's preparing vegetables I don't like, I'm to come and make my own. "But you have to eat them," she warns. "If you try to cheat, we go right back to square one, you eat whatever I prepare."

"OK."

"Deal," she says, the way she usually does after one of her "negotiations". "Shake hands."

I hate that, but I have no choice, so I shake.

Well, that Saturday she calls me in the kitchen to make carrot salad for myself because she's fixing cabbage for dinner. I make the salad and put it in the fridge and forget to eat it.

Mildred pounces – I cheated, I better eat that salad right-right now because her food isn't going to waste. She watches me like a hawk while I eat the horrible mess, so I don't get a chance to spit it out through the kitchen window. Underneath the kitchen window is a whole tomato orchard where I used to spit at dinner. Mildred discovered I was wasting her tomatoes when she saw the bigtime orchard growing there. She got mad. I thought she should be grateful, getting a whole set of tomatoes for free when they could easily have passed through my stomach into the toilet instead.

So you see the kind of unreasonable woman Mildred was. Everything had to be perfect.

Verene hated her too but Verene said we had to behave ourselves, because if we didn't Mildred would throw us out on the streets, and Mummy couldn't come back from America to save us because her papers weren't straight, and where would we be if that happened? Plus we didn't want Mummy to be fretting. If she was fretting, she might have a nervous breakdown and not be able to work and earn enough money to come get us away from dread Mildred.

Verene and me started living with Mildred two years now, when Mummy went to America and Verene was twelve and I was nine going on ten. My six other aunts had a hundred children and no money, so they couldn't keep us. Plus they didn't live near any good high schools. Mildred was terribly educated and she lived in the city where there were oodles of good schools. She was an auditing manager. That's why she kept auditing us.

"Your Aunt Mildred is the best person to take care of you," our mother said. "She wi' bring you up right and make you somebody."

"SHE WILL CUT OUT OUR LIVER AND EAT US RAW!" I shouted. "How you can send us to live with that woman?"

"Brenda, watch your manners," my mother said sternly. "It's your aunt you're talking about." She tried to bribe me by saying, "Don't worry, it's only for a short time. As soon as I get settled I send for you."

I screamed and tore my clothes and spit on myself and went on as bad as I could, I even went childish and prayed to die so they would all be sorry and I would go to my own funeral and watch them dying of sorrow. But nothing worked. My mother packed us up like parcels, and off we went to Mildred in her big house in Cherry Gardens.

At first it looked like things mightn't be so bad. She let us watch TV and do what we wanted. She even tried to be friendly. *Friendly* is a word that don't plant peas at Mildred's fence, so when I say *friendly* you have to understand I mean relatively speaking. Anyways, at first Verene and me thought she mightn't be so bad.

That was the first day.

Caranapung! The second day Mildred starts laying down the rules. She's all sweet and sugary, saying we can discuss them, but you know that's just a front. Rules to kill! No TV on weekdays except cartoons up to four o'clock, homework and bed for me by eight-thirty, nine-thirty for Verene. Wash your underwear every morning and hang it outside to dry. Make sure it's in the sun. Clean your room and scrub your bathtub every Saturday morning. Wash up after meals. No dirty dishes overnight in the sink. Church on Sundays. Any friends you have calling or visiting, Mildred has to meet them. No sleeping over at anybody's house, and anybody coming to sleep over at ours, Mildred has to meet their parents first. She isn't sure she'll let us go to parties, but if she does, it's weekends only. Plus she's checking out the party and dropping us and picking us up herself by ten o'clock. *Ten o'clock!*

Whew! Gestapo! Lady Dracula!

And Mildred was only warming up. Every day

more rules came tumbling out the closet. Rules about vegetables. Rules about no junk food, and fruit juice and water only. Rules about what kinds of TV shows you could and couldn't watch. Some of those I didn't mind, like the rule about not watching soap operas because of the sex. Sex was stupid and boring anyhow. But she made me stop watching horror and war. It was bad for my subconscious, Mildred said. Life became one boring round of *Sesame Street* and *National Geographic*.

We couldn't go on school trips to anywhere there was water, like a beach or a river. Mildred said we might drown.

Mildred's idea of fun was for us to go out with *her* on Friday nights. We'd drive to Holborn Road and buy jerk chicken and festival and pretend to sit and eat and talk like family. Most of the time Mildred was hurrying and rushing us to get ready, so that killed all the fun – if there was any fun in the first place. Verene said, "Aunt Mildred, who ever heard of hurrying to relax?"

Mildred hurried anyway.

Afterwards we went to the video store and

139

rented two movies and pigged out on the floor in front of the TV with peanuts and cashews and maybe cake. That part was kind of OK except that Mildred sat with us wearing her dread face that couldn't smile, and though we got to pick the videos we had to pick according to her rules.

She killed us with homework. Verene didn't mind because she's a nerd, but I'm no Verene.

One time Mildred was harassing me about going to the library to work on a project that wasn't due for ages – a whole week!

"Real parents know how to treat their children as individuals," I said. "You can't expect me to be doing homework all the time like Verene. Man must have some fun."

Boy, Mildred got mad. She grabbed me in my shirt collar and snarled, "Look here, little girl. You see me, I am a parent by default. I not prepared for this, so I am the first to admit I just guessing and spelling. But I bringing you up by my lights, not by your lights, so I don't care which fancy movie you see *that* foolishness in. I not no movie parent, I is a Jamaican aunt, and if you give me any more of your lip I corn you good and proper."

It was the first I ever heard Mildred cuss instead of trying to explain the rules. I must admit, it nearly nervoused me.

I wrote and told my mother everything this witch-woman was doing to us. I told her she better hurry up and come for us before it was too late and she would find only our carcasses. I made sure to embroider things a bit so she could see it was really b-a-a-a-d.

My mother never answered our letters.

"Don't think she's abandoned us," Verene said, chewing her bottom lip and screwing up her face the way she did when she was worried. "I think she just not straight yet and maybe she scared to write in case the Immigration people intercept her letters and come after her."

Gosh, for a girl of fourteen, Verene could be so dumb sometimes. "Of course Mummy write us," I said scornfully. "You think I stupid? Not a thing but Mildred hide our letters that Mummy send."

"Shhh," Verene said. "She might hear you."

We began putting school as our return address.

We still didn't get any reply.

Mildred was really smart. "Not a thing but she go to the principal and tell her to give her any letters that come to us," I explained to my poor naïve sister. But you have to understand, Verene only book-bright, she really not that smart. She didn't believe me, and even worried that our mother had died.

But the truth was nagging at her brainpan and finally it came out, just like that. Like a worm boring through a pretty mango skin.

It happened like this. Verene wanted to go to her class fête and Mildred said no. "I hear of all the goings-on at those class parties and I not sending you anywhere," Mildred said. "You forget the principal had to cancel that same class fête last year when she saw the goings-on?"

Verene is a girl who don't talk or quarrel, but she just exploded. You could see she had been keeping a lot in. "Aunt Mildred, I am not a prisoner and you are not my keeper!" she shouted. "And you are not my mother. I don't belong to you; you are NOT my mother."

Aunt Mildred gave her a dry look. "I am well aware of that, but you still not going to any fête."

Verene burst into tears. "You think this is the Dark Ages? Why you want to keep us prisoner? Is the same way you hide Mummy's letters and don't give them to us."

Mildred went very still. If it wasn't for the sound of Verene crying, you could have heard a pin drop.

"Is that what you think?" Mildred said at last, in a voice so quiet even I got almost nervous. "You think your mother has been writing to you and I have been hiding her letters?"

But Verene just ran into our room and slammed the door. Mildred stood there looking into space for a long time, then she said to the room, "I don't even know where Perlette is. I haven't heard from her since the first week she went over." And she walked out.

Verene decided she should apologize for her wrongful accusation, but I wasn't so easily fooled. I started to chant down Mildred every night before bed.

The funny thing about Mildred though – and I have to tell you this because I don't want to be unfair – is that no matter what, you could depend on her. I suppose people who love to set rules have to be like that, don't they? Or they'd ruin their reputations.

My other aunts were awfully nice, but, like most grownups, totally undependable. But with Mildred, you could put a pot on the fire not knowing where the food was coming from, and one minute before the water boiled, there she would be with the food.

Like the time I was in prep school and a hurricane was coming and all the schools sent over the radio telling parents and guardians to come for their children. Our teachers made us pack our things while they huddled around the radio listening to what was going on. It was chaos downtown and traffic wasn't getting through. Then the sky went scary and breeze started to blow. A boy in my class named Sean started to cry because he thought his parents mightn't come for him and he would be killed. I tried to cheer him up.

"Don't worry," I said. "Even if your parents

don't come, my aunt wi' come and she wi' give you a lift home."

We waited and waited and Mildred was one of the first parents coming through the gate, carrying her oversized handbag that she brought the office home in, holding it like she was going to put some children in it for safekeeping. She had stopped on the way to collect Verene from high school. She took Sean home and dropped us off and wheeled her car around and went to collect the children of friends who had no cars and were stranded downtown. She never said anything, but in the night when the storm was raging she made us hot chocolate and we sat on her bed.

At times like that I almost liked Mildred. But sooner or later she went back to her evil ways.

Still, when you've lived as long as me, you realize nothing goes on for ever. Finally my chants against Mildred worked and Mummy came. She came early one morning when we should have been in school, but Mildred said we could skip school because she was coming. We went to the airport and I was so excited I almost wet myself. I squeezed my hands in my lap and tried not to wriggle, but I couldn't help it, I wriggled all the way. I threw words about what I would and would not do when I got to America. I felt almost friendly towards Aunt Mildred. "No more raw vegetables and water, Aunt Mildred," I said, laughing. "Kentucky Fried Chicken and soda like riches."

"Hmm, how nice for you," Mildred said. "I hope you enjoy yourself."

I leant over the back of Verene's seat and breathed loudly through my mouth because I knew it would annoy Mildred. "Don't worry, I go send some for you through the post office," I said.

"Thanks, but I'll pass," Mildred said in that disgusting matter-of-fact voice. Verene put up her hand without looking and pushed me hard in my forehead, so that I fell back in my seat. "Can't you shut up?" she hissed. She was sitting there with her face screwed up. I wondered what she was thinking, but with Verene you never know.

When our mother came through the barrier we hardly recognized her, she'd changed so much. Her skin was much paler, like she'd been bleached, and she sort of looked polished up, real hotshot, if you know what I mean. She wore a real snazzy pants outfit in black leather and lots of jewellery. Verene ran and hugged her and started bawling, right there in the airport in front of everybody. Like she was at a wake instead of greeting her mum whom she hadn't seen in, I mean, years. Can you imagine? I didn't know where to look.

To make up for Verene's childish behaviour, I just smiled and waited for Mummy to hug me, though I was dying of impatience inside. She hugged me tight, but when she let go Mildred grabbed and kissed her and I stood there feeling foolish, like I was Mildred and Mildred was me. I didn't know Mildred could hug and kiss anybody and I was vexed that she did all that while I'd just waited for Mummy to hug me. I had only done it to restore some dignity to the way our family was looking, with Verene bawling and washing away the whole airport.

Anyways, to cut a long story short, because I really don't want to dwell on all that, we drove home, my mother sitting in the front seat with

Mildred, and me and Verene in the back. The whole way Mummy and Mildred were talking and talking and Mummy kept turning and twisting around in her seat to look at us and hug our heads (since she couldn't get to the rest of us), exclaiming how glad she was to see us and asking all sorts of questions about how we were doing in school, and had we been good girls and not given Auntie Mildred any trouble, and did we know how wonderful it had been for Auntie Mildred to take us and look after us so nice?

I couldn't believe my ears. Whose side was she on, for goodness' sake? I mean, were we her daughters or weren't we? Not a word about why she hadn't written to us and why she'd let Mildred drink our blood like Dracula. Instead there she was thanking awful Mildred over and over for looking after us and Mildred looking pious and murmuring like some sort of saint, "You don't need to thank me, Perlette, it was no trouble. I was glad to do it." I glared at my mother's headback and decided then and there that I might as well run away. There was no justice in the world of grownups.

That night after we had sat up very late, our mother came to our room and sat on our bed and hugged us and cried all over again and said how glad she was to see us, and how much she loved us and would never leave us again. And how she hadn't written because for a long time she was hiding from Immigration and couldn't get any good-paying job, and she was so ashamed she didn't have anything to send, and she didn't want to send a letter with no money in it, but she knew Mildred would take care of us.

"So when we going to America?" I asked, interrupting this endless flow. Verene wasn't saying anything.

"Well, it might take another couple of months to get your papers sorted out. That's why I came home, to sort out the last bits and pieces. But soon, soon." She laughed, very shiftily. I decided not to trust her at all.

But in the end our papers really did come through and we were on our way to the airport in Mildred's Mercedes-Benz with our luggage and our mother.

At the barrier Mildred hugged and kissed our mother and Verene, and to my surprise Verene hugged her back real tight and whispered – I could swear that's what I heard – "Thank you for everything, Aunt Mildred." Well, what do you know? Talk about traitors.

Mildred turned to me and held out her hand and smiled her tight constipation smile. I guess when you have a face like Mildred's it's an awful chore to smile. "Shake, Brenda?" she said.

I shrugged. "OK." I shook.

Mildred suddenly let go of my hand and hugged me so tight I thought I would choke. "Take care of yourself, and God bless," she whispered in a choky voice like Verene.

Then she let me go and said to my mother, "Talk to you, Perlette," and walked to her car without looking back and drove away.

I was so embarrassed I didn't know where to look.

Afterwards when we are sitting in the plane waiting for take-off, I look through my window and see all the people waving to their people in the plane. I know Mildred isn't among them because I saw her get in her car with my own two eyes. But still I wonder if it's her I see there in the beige suit among the wavers on the waving deck. I know it can't be, but Mildred must have got in amongst me real bad without me realizing, because always afterwards when I remember her, I remember her hugging me tight at the airport and then walking away not looking back, and coming through the school gate with her oversized handbag like she was going to put me in it, that time there was the hurricane and she came for me and took Sean home.

I guess I might write to her after all, I think as the plane lifts off.

But don't get me wrong, I'm not saying I will. Just that I might think about it.

THE BOY
WHO WENT THROUGH THE
PAGES OF A BOOK

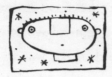

Once upon a time there was Oscar Barrett.

Oscar was a small, skinny boy whom no one noticed because he seemed to be hardly ever there. And indeed, if the truth be told, he wasn't.

Oscar was a boy who lived a double life. At school he was this nerdy-looking, double-jointed, undersized midge in oversized glasses, who sat quiet as a mouse in his corner at the back of the classroom and didn't live up to his nerdy looks at all, since he got mediocre grades in everything. He had a medium black skin, medium black eyes, a medium ugly face, and all in all was so ordinary and medium that nobody even bothered to tease him. At PE, when they played rough games like football, they pushed him carelessly out of the way where he stood on the sidelines. All boys had to present themselves at PE. Oscar presented himself, but either he couldn't play or the other boys didn't let him play. They called him Mouso, for Mouse or Mousy.

A new PE teacher came who didn't understand about ignoring Mouso because he was so medium and ordinary. The teacher said, "Boy, you can't just stand on the sidelines, you need to grow some muscles. Here!" And he threw the ball at Oscar. Oscar did his best to catch it, but it slipped through his hands, bounced on the ground, flew in the air and hit the teacher on his bald head. The class roared with laughter.

"Atta boy, Mouso!" they shouted, but he hadn't done it on purpose. Oscar was frantic that the teacher might think he had done it on purpose. He opened his mouth, shrinking, to explain sorry sir, but it wasn't on purpose, please sir. But the class didn't give him a chance. Delighted that Mouso had some guts in him after all, they pulled him into the game and for the next half-hour he found himself pushed and battered and bruised between boy and ball.

"Here, Mouso!"

"Whack it, Mouso!"

"Wahhhh, Mouso!"

In the exuberant joy of the game they jostled and leapt all over him with their large bodies. Their shouts echoed like bells in the hills under which the schoolhouse sat. Their joy made Oscar feel like an old man, too old for his classmates and his years.

They changed his nickname to Coco, because a huge coco came up on the teacher's bald head where Oscar had hit him, and they felt that such a heroic deed deserved commendation. To them, nicknames were not a way of making you feel like an outsider. Nicknames were a way of laughing and belonging, and remembering famous things like putting a coco on the teacher's head. Oscar was too weary to protest any more that he hadn't meant it. And by the next day he didn't care.

All his life at school felt so dead, it had no shine. Only sometimes, in history class, when they taught about heroes, he dreamt that he would be a great hero and save the world, and then his soul took fire within him, and his eyes sparkled and blazed with an inner light. But soon his soul's fire died, for he looked at himself and he thought, How could I be a hero? He was too meagre and medium to save the world. He felt, oh, so betwixt and between. Like a kite caught on a lamppost, flapping, but unable to fly.

The only time Oscar felt alive was when he was in his room with his nose buried in a book of his own choosing. Not the books he had to read for school, but the ones he saved up his pocket money to buy, or the ones he borrowed from the branch library, where the mobile library brought new books every second Friday. You could borrow any books that came, but you could also order any books you wanted, and the van would bring them, neatly packaged in brown paper with your name and address on, to separate them from the books that anyone could have.

Oscar ordered all the books whose names he'd found on the jackets of the ones he'd read. His neatly wrapped brown parcels, arriving in the van every second Friday, made him feel like somebody, like he was noticed and important. He read every kind of story-book you could think of: books for small people and books for grownups; books about here and books about there; books about sea voyages and books on land; books for laughing and some for crying over; books with poetry, where the sentences staggered and leapt and ran; and books with straight sentences, commas and stops. He didn't understand some of the things he read, but what he understood drew him into a world of mystery and excitement where words were their own magic.

Mostly he loved books of fantasy because they made him think there really was another world, with other people, where he had come from and where he truly belonged. A magical world totally different from the dreadful, ordinary one in which he was forced to live. Oscar didn't feel he belonged to his parents. He thought he might have been a changeling. He thought so because the world around him felt so fuzzed and shadowy, like the background of pictures, while the worlds he read about in books were clearer than the most vivid of photographs, and full of light.

But mostly he thought he was a changeling because his parents didn't approve of his reading.

"Reading story-book again?" his father said, looking exasperated, whenever he came into Oscar's room. "Boy, I don't understand you. Man must read sensible book, book 'bout life, history and politics and thing, not foolishness 'bout fairy and huge beast and toad a-talk and dem nonsense. Cha."

His father loaded him with books about history and politics and thing, but Oscar found them heavy and hard, and could not read them. "They have no fire," he whispered to himself, looking out through windows into the real magical world he saw in his mind from far away. "I want magic."

But he didn't want to hurt his father's feelings so he kept the books and tried his best.

His mother said, "Bruce, he not ready yet. When he get older he will read them," but you could see she didn't believe it because she looked worried and sent Oscar to play football. "Boy must look and think like boy, not girl," she told him. "Need some muscles in your body and your mind."

He was no good at football, so his mother sighed and looked more worried.

Oscar had a book, *Fairy Tales From Around the World*. In it were stories from faraway places – Norway, Lapland, Alaska, Asia – so he knew these places had doors and windows through which you could pass into the magic world where he was born. But where he lived, in the Caribbean, had been sealed up without doors, for there were no stories from there in that book or any other book of magical tales that he had seen.

People in country yards where Oscar lived told stories on moonshine nights while children played with ackee seeds in a moon-silvered ring. Stories about Whooping Boy, who lost his face in the world's wild winds, and Three Foot Horse, who pawed the earth on midnight roads so you couldn't pass; and Rolling Calf with his clanking chain, who breathed fire through his nostrils and stopped you at the crossroads with a cruel ball of gold; and Old Higue, who shed her old woman's skin and fooled young men in dreams like she was a beautiful maiden; and River Mumma, who was a guardian of the ways, and Anancy the Trickster Man, who knew all trades. Oscar knew these stories that people told in their yards. But they were not stories in books, and so he found in them no joy.

But Oscar's life was about to change for ever.

The teacher whose head he had put the coco on started paying him great attention. He called Oscar and said do or die, you have to play football. You're too meagre and too medium. I'm putting you on the DaCosta house team.

The teacher meant it about playing football, but he didn't mean it about the house team. He only said that to show Oscar how serious he was.

Oscar was so frightened, he stood shivering and waiting to die. But he didn't die, so he went instead to the library to find a book to hide in.

"Oh, hi Oscar," the librarian said, smiling. Oscar was her favourite customer because he read all the old musty books that the main library kept dumping in her branch and no one else wanted to read. He made her library look like it was prospering. "Here's a new book I was saving for you. Just the kind you like."

It was a flat, shiny book with *Dreamtales From Around the Caribbean* written in looping gold letters across the bright red cover. Inside were pictures like fairy tales. Oscar stared. He hadn't known such a book existed.

"It's new," the librarian said. "Just came out."

He took it and hurried home.

He didn't get to start reading until night, as he had chores to do. There seemed to be more chores than usual, and by the time he'd finished Oscar was very tired. But he was determined to look into this strange new book which said in its title that there was magic right there where he lived. He sat in his bed, drew up the covers, opened the book to the first story, and began to read.

"Once upon a time," he read, his spine tingling at the familiar, magical words... And then the strangest thing happened. The words began to dip and dance so that he couldn't see. Oscar grabbed the book to prevent it slipping to the floor. But instead of steadying the book, his hand began to rock up and down, up and down, like a leaf on a wave.

And indeed it seemed that the book and then the bed had become waves in the sea, for they were heaving and rolling and surging up towards the ceiling and down again like seawater when a storm was coming or a boat's keel had cut the waves. Oscar felt himself heaving on the crest of this sea. He tried to cry out, but couldn't. Then there was a rushing sound and his ears filled with wind. At the same time, his eyes went blind, and this time he did scream, "EEEEEEEEEEEE!!!", and the whole world blotted out.

When he opened his eyes he was lying in grass before some wooden steps. A door above the steps opened and a woman came out. Oscar sat up and stared. Her hair was in bright orange dreadlocks that stuck up all over her head. She had only one eye, right in the middle of her forehead. It was a bright, jewel green. Her skin was brown-red like mahogany, and she was wearing a long flowing dress that rippled like seawater and changed colour each time it rippled, shades of blue and green and violet like the sea. She was beautiful.

"Hello, Oscar," she said, holding out her hand. "Won't you come in?" Her voice whispered like water swishing in caves.

Wondering, delighted, Oscar went in.

Her house was dark and shadowy, so he couldn't see anything properly. It was a strange, shining dark that made him think of riverbanks with moss and ferns and thickly growing trees that overhung the water. Glimpses of soft and wonderful colours shifted and shimmered in the dark, so light and fleeting he wondered if he imagined them all.

"Who are you? What is your name?" he whispered. In this house, nothing seemed right but whispers.

The lady smiled. "That is not important as yet, Oscar. What is important is you."

Oscar's eyes grew. "Me?" he squeaked. Nobody had ever thought him important before, nobody outside his home, that is. "Are you my real mother?"

The lady laughed, and did not answer. Her laugh was like her voice; a whisper, a sigh, water lapping.

She just said, "Sit down, Oscar," and gestured. Oscar found himself sitting in a soft seat he could not see, nor remember how he got there. The lady sat across from him. His seat rose and fell, rose and fell, like a water rocking-chair.

"So, Mr Oscar, why have you come to see me?"

Oscar was surprised. He didn't think that he had come; it was more like he had been kidnapped. Yet he found himself hurtling into speech.

"I have to play football. Mr Hosein says I have to play tomorrow. Everyone will laugh at me."

The lady's eyebrow rose. "But why?" she asked, smiling.

"Because I'm skinny and clumsy and—" Oscar searched for words to describe his inadequacy "—and medium," he finished, and hung his head in shame.

The lady looked at him thoughtfully. "And do

you want to play football, Oscar Barrett?"

The question surprised Oscar. Come to think of it, he had never thought of it at all, he had just assumed he didn't.

"Yes," he said, sounding shocked. "Yes, I do want to play. But I'm always scared I'll do stupidness and fail."

The lady didn't answer that one. Instead she asked, "May I offer you something to eat?"

Oscar discovered that he was ravenously hungry, though he had eaten quite a bit at dinner. It seemed like his life was full of discoveries all of a sudden. "Yes please," he said in his new voice of surprise.

The lady made another gesture, too quick for Oscar to notice what she did. All he knew was that a gleaming round table, shining like gold, suddenly appeared in front of him. It was a very strange-looking table. On its top sprouted long grass and golden leaves, like it was a garden.

"What would you like to eat?" the lady asked.

Oscar stammered, feeling shy. He didn't want to appear greedy.

"Anything you want," the lady said gently.

He thought of hamburgers (in that way Oscar was just like other children), but thought maybe the lady wouldn't have that kind of food in her house, seeing as it was a real magic house and not a junk food mall. But before he could think of what else to ask for, the lady clapped her hands over the table and said, "Hamburger, table."

Lo and behold! A plateful of hamburger and the most luscious, steaming hot chips Oscar had ever seen appeared among the tall grass and golden leaves. Beside it, a beaker of cane juice, just the drink Oscar always thought of when he thought of hamburgers.

"Eat, Oscar," the lady said, smiling, and she sat back in her chair and began to eat also. She plucked and ate the grass on the tabletop, like a horse. Her face flickered and shimmered in sea-rainbow colours, and Oscar thought how in her hands the grass looked remarkably like seaweed.

It was the best hamburger Oscar had ever tasted. He ate it so fast that he burped. His face grew hot with shame. The lady only smiled, her one green eye beaming down on him gently, kindly.

"Your table," Oscar said, stammering. "It's just like Anancy's big jester pot in the story. He told the pot what to cook and the pot cooked it all up in a jiffy. He wasn't supposed to wash the pot or the magic wouldn't work, but his wife didn't know and she washed the pot and there was no more magic and Anancy was in a rage." He finished very fast, wondering if he was talking too much.

The lady laughed; water gurgling, rippling. "Of course and indeed," she said gaily. "Anancy got that pot from me." Then she frowned. "Ah, but I forget. You are not impressed with Anancy. You find him boring."

Oscar stared, suddenly shocked to realize he didn't think like that any more.

"Everything seems so different down here," he whispered.

"Even Anancy?" The lady's eye was twinkling, like she was laughing at him, but only a little.

"Yes," Oscar said. And again, crying out, "Yes!"

He looked at the lady with pained eyes. "He'll be ordinary again when I go back – up there." And then he whispered almost like beseeching, begging the lady not to let it be so. "Won't he?"

"Hmm. Maybe he will and maybe he won't," the lady said. She sat rocking and rocking, her seat going up and down like the sea.

At last she said, "Suppose Anancy came from faraway lands, from over the sea, like the winds and the snows of north and east, or trailing light from the storehouses of the sun – would you still have thought he was ordinary, up there?"

"I would have thought he was wonderful!" the boy cried, his heart aching with the picture of beautiful things the lady's words conjured.

"You would? Ah, indeed and you would."

The lady fell silent a while. She sat, rocking, her seat lifting up and going down like Oscar's, like waves. Her face and her dress shimmered and shadowed, shadowed and shimmered, just like light on water under sun-dappled leaves. Finally she said, "Perhaps the stories in books feel magical only because they are far away, and the ones around you feel ordinary because they are near. The secret is to find a way to make what is ordinary become magical."

"How can you do that?" Oscar was fascinated, but puzzled.

"You have to look with magic eyes," the lady said, and Oscar shivered. "The magic is always there. You just have to believe it's there. Then you will see it. It's like playing football, Oscar," she said.

"Playing football?"

"Yes. Come, let me show you." And she rose and took him by the hand and led him to a black space in the room which he thought at first was a hole, but as his eyes grew accustomed to the dark there, he realized it was a window-pane made of a solid sheet of black glass. "Touch it," the lady said, and her voice cast a spell, and Oscar reached out his hand and touched the black glass and it became a mirror. It started to wrinkle and shimmer and buck like it was calypsoing underwater. The black rolled away like a great door unfolding and he found himself looking into his schoolyard.

The schoolyard was alive with laughter and shouting and boys in their red and yellow PE shirts. The air was bright and golden and new. A crowd milled around three boys carrying a fourth boy on their shoulders, and the fourth boy was laughing and holding a glittering football trophy high above his head.

Oscar's mouth dropped open when he heard what they were chanting.

"Coco, Coco, Coco, Coco! Coco is our champion, we know so, know so, know so!"

And the boy they were carrying was himself, laughing and red-shirted and free. The mirror rolled again, like camera footage, and he saw himself on the football pitch. There were two teams on the pitch, his school team and the school which he knew to be the reigning team, and hundreds of boys and people with flags were waving and screaming in the stands: "Coco, Coco, Coco! He go beat you an' you know so!"

And he was dribbling the ball past the reigning team, wriggling in and out of feet like magic, like Didi, like Pelé, like Garrincha, and racing towards the goalpost and dodging the goalie who came out to stop him but fell sprawling on his bum in the mud instead; and there was himself – "Oscar, Oscar, what a knuckleduster!" – putting the ball in the back of the net with a kick like singing, and the referee's whistle was blowing and hordes in gold and scarlet were swarming onto the pitch screaming and mad with joy.

The picture rolled backwards and back and back, and as it went back, the blackness rolled forward, until the window was still, and just glass once more.

Oscar stood there, tears running down his cheeks. The lady's eye shimmered into his. "And you thought you were ordinary," she said. "Yet you have eyes to see magic. Indeed and indeed, Oscar Barrett, all you have to do is believe it."

"But how can I believe it?" he whispered. "It's just a dream."

"It only looks that way," the lady said. "But really and truly, it is love."

"Love?" Oscar echoed, not understanding.

"Yes, love. What you saw in the mirror is what you always dreamt, isn't it? But you were too scared to let anybody know."

"Yes," he said.

The lady said, "Every time you dream of being

special, it's your heart loving yourself. Don't hide from your dreams, Oscar Barrett. Believe them. And then the magic door will open for you."

"Yes," Oscar whispered, beginning to understand.

"But you have to want it badly enough." She sounded almost stern. "This is not for playing around with."

"No," Oscar said.

"So" – the lady led him back to his seat – "you are no ordinary boy at all, at all, Oscar Barrett. Not medium. *Rare*."

Oscar thought his heart would burst with love for the lady. "You're special!" he cried. "I want to put you in a book. You and Anancy and all the others, so everybody can see."

She smiled her sun-water-dappled smile. "Ah. Then you must study hard, and learn words. Every day you must learn new words, and believe. Those who make the magic books, they live in the same ordinary world as everybody else. And their stories are about the ordinary things around them. But they have learnt the secret of weaving words so others can see the magic that is there all the time."

And as she spoke, it seemed to Oscar that her words made a shimmer of light that wove and twisted itself until it was a bright tapestry of many colours. The tapestry swung in the dimness, then softly withdrew and disappeared.

"Come, Oscar Barrett," the lady said, suddenly sounding brisk. "Time for you to go home."

And Oscar's chair began to lilt faster than ever, heaving and tossing like a boat, and the house was breaking up like the sea at high tide. When he looked for the lady she was standing in a great fountain of water; water was sprouting from her hair, which had turned into great knotted roots of trees, and the water from the fountain was falling into a churning pool that rippled out and joined the sea. In the water she had no feet, but a long, graceful fin.

And in the midst of the sea the gold table from which he had fed was dancing and bobbing, then it spun in a circle and disappeared.

"What is your name?" he cried, and she cried back, but he could not hear because of the thunder in his ears. He closed his eyes tight as water covered his head.

When he opened them he was in his bed, the book in bright gold and scarlet on his knees. Oscar read the print on the page at which the book was open. "They call me River Mumma," it said, "who guards the riverheads going down to the sea."

Oscar straightened the book and began to read. But he was very tired, and soon he fell asleep.

The next morning, Oscar went onto the football pitch. After many falls, bruises, jeers, teasings and wonderful encounters over many days, he made the house team.

Many years later, a little boy picked a book off a library shelf. *Dreamtales From Around the Caribbean Volume Two*, by Oscar Barrett, the scarlet and gold cover said. And inside the cover was magic and singing and light, like someone had looked into the world with love.